unforgettable

it girl novels created by Cecily von Ziegesar:

The It Girl
Notorious
Reckless
Unforgettable

If you like **the it girl**, you may also enjoy:

Bass Ackwards and Belly Up by Elizabeth Craft and Sarah Fain
Secrets of My Hollywood Life by Jen Calonita
Haters by Alisa Valdes-Rodriguez

and keep your eye out for
Betwixt by Tara Bray Smith, coming October 2007

unforgettable

an it girl novel

CREATED BY
CECILY VON ZIEGESAR

 LITTLE, BROWN AND COMPANY
New York ❧ Boston

Little, Brown and Company
Hachette Book Group USA
1271 Avenue of the Americas, New York, NY 10020
Visit our Web site at www.lb-teens.com

First Edition: November 2007

Produced by Alloy Entertainment
151 West 26th Street, New York, NY 10001

ISBN-13: 978-0-316-11348-9
ISBN-10: 0-316-11348-4

10 9 8 7 6 5 4 3 2 1
CWO
Printed in the United States of America

unforgettable

Most people were raised to believe they are just as good as the next person. I was always told I was better.

—Katharine Hepburn

**A WAVERLY OWL KNOWS GOOD THINGS DON'T
ALWAYS COME TO THOSE WHO WAIT.
REALLY, WHO HAS THE PATIENCE?**

Jenny Humphrey stepped out of Jameson House after portraiture class and took in a breath of crisp fall air. Two tall, lanky senior guys in cargo pants and Waverly sweatshirts were tossing a Frisbee around on the lush green quad. They paused as she passed, and Jenny felt herself blushing. She walked away quickly, the fallen leaves crackling beneath her mustard-yellow suede ballet flats, wishing more than almost anything that she were headed down Amsterdam Avenue with her dad to get a couple of vanilla buttercream cupcakes from the Viennese bakery around the corner from their Upper West Side apartment. All she wanted was to get lost on the streets of Manhattan among millions of strangers, none of whom would look at her and think, *There goes the girl Easy Walsh is about to dump.*

Jenny tugged at the hem of her short gray wool Anthroplogie miniskirt. She'd spent a little extra time getting ready today, anticipating seeing Easy for the first time since Saturday's disastrous party while the Dumbarton girls were all supposed to be on lockdown. She wore a pair of dark pin-striped Wolford tights that made her legs look longer than they were and a black RL button-down with three-quarter-length sleeves that made her chest look smaller than it was. But then Easy hadn't even bothered to show up for class. Jenny's heart had sunk when Mrs. Silver closed the door to the studio and Easy's almost-black curly mop was nowhere to be found. What did that mean? Was he actually *avoiding* her?

She hadn't spoken with Easy since the terrible revelation—during a very public game of I Never on Saturday night, no less—that he had taken Callie Vernon, her unbearably tall, skinny, beautiful roommate who just happened to be his ex-girlfriend, out to an intimate dinner with his father. Not only had he *not* invited Jenny, his supposed girlfriend, he hadn't even *told* her about it, though apparently half the world already knew. And then the rest of the world found out after Tinsley "Definition of Pure Evil" Carmichael broke the news to an entire roomful of happily partying Waverly Owls during the I Never game.

Easy had e-mailed Jenny on Saturday night after the party disastrously disbanded, asking if she wanted to talk, but she'd written back and said she wasn't ready—she needed to figure out what the hell she was feeling first. But even having said that, she couldn't help hoping he would try to sneak in to see

her with a handful of wildflowers or slip one of his goofy cari-
catures into her student mailbox. She didn't want to be one of
those girls who said the exact opposite of what she meant, but
still—it would have been nice to see Easy try.

Suddenly something sharp hit Jenny in the back of the neck,
and she whirled around, expecting to see one of the Frisbee guys
rushing toward her apologetically. But instead, a white paper
airplane made of thick watercolor paper lay on the cobblestone
path near her feet. She picked it up and unfolded it, her heart
starting to thud in her chest, but nothing was written inside.

"Psst!" She glanced toward the cluster of birch trees to the
left of Jameson House. There, nestled among them, a yellow
leaf stuck behind his ear, was the boy she couldn't stop thinking about. Easy's enormous dark blue eyes looked nervous as he
motioned her over.

Jenny shuffled slowly in his direction, a vision of Easy sitting across a candlelit dinner table from Callie and his father,
chatting and laughing, flashing across her brain. She started
to feel a little queasy and tried to replace the image with the
memory of Sunday, when she'd hung out in the Dumbarton
common room with Brett and Kara and even, surprisingly
enough, *Callie.* They'd all complained about boys—no specif-
ics, just general, feel-good, boy-dissing bonding. *It wasn't that
long ago they were swinging from trees, reaching for their bananas,*
Callie had declared, and then they'd all made monkey noises
the rest of the night. Now, seeing Easy among the leafy branches, Jenny had to suppress an *ooooh ooooh eeeeee eeeee!*

"Hey," she said instead.

Easy's smile fell, as if he had been expecting a friendlier greeting, and Jenny felt herself softening. "Why are you hiding in the bushes?" She raised an eyebrow.

He stepped out from the thatch of trees, glancing around. Easy was wearing a Waverly rugby shirt covered in grass stains, and his normally bright eyes were a little bloodshot, as if he hadn't been sleeping well. Well, it was only fair that he'd have trouble sleeping—she'd been tossing and turning for the past three nights, visions of tall, gorgeous Easy and tall, gorgeous Callie plaguing her brain.

"Didn't want Silver to see me." He rubbed a hand over his eyes. "I told her I was sick."

"Then why are you here?" Jenny couldn't help but blurt out.

Easy's dark blue eyes clouded over. "I . . . don't know. I guess I just wanted to talk to you."

"Oh." Jenny fumbled through her bag for her brandless white aviators that she'd bought on the street in SoHo before school had started. It was sunny out, but mostly she didn't want Easy to be able to see exactly what she was thinking. Her brother, Dan, used to tell her that her face was about as hard to read as a stop sign. After rustling through her disorganized bag without any luck, she stopped searching, not wanting to accidentally unearth a tampon or something equally embarrassing. Instead, she shaded her eyes as she glanced up. "Wanna walk me back to the dorm? I've got to get ready for practice." He nodded slowly and they turned in the direction of Dumbarton.

They walked side by side down the cobblestone path, the

shouts of students at sports practices in the distance ringing through the clean autumn air. They were both silent for a few minutes, and Jenny became painfully aware of the enormous space between them. Easy walked just out of her reach, and she had no idea what he was thinking. She wanted to turn and tackle him into a pile of leaves and kiss him, but she just . . . couldn't. She started to dig through her bag again, at last finding the sunglasses. She untangled them from the Owl pendant key chain she'd bought at the little shop in Rhinecliff that sold all things Waverly and slipped the aviators on her face.

A pack of girls in plaid miniskirts and kneesocks huddling on the library steps stared at them as they passed. All of Waverly had been buzzing with the revelations from the I Never game on Saturday night—there was Tinsley Carmichael, and Brett Messerschmidt's unmasked virginity to discuss, not to mention the revelation that Jeremiah Mortimer, Brett's longtime boyfriend, was suddenly *not* a virgin, and neither was the pretty blond St. Lucius girl who had mysteriously followed him over to Dumbarton. And of course the fact that Easy Walsh had sneaked out on a date with Callie Vernon behind Jenny's back. The fact that Alison Quentin and Alan St. Girard had hooked up at the party seemed totally banal in comparison and ranked relatively low on the Waverly gossip meter, even though hookups usually received top billing.

Easy shuffled his feet as they walked along. "I just . . . wanted to apologize. Again."

Jenny sighed. She *knew* he was sorry. But that didn't really mean anything. Sorry about what? That he'd taken Callie out to dinner instead of her? That he'd hurt and embarrassed her? That he'd completely messed things up between them?

Or was he sorry because he knew he was going to break her heart?

Jenny stopped walking. She'd overheard some girls in her English class talking about how they'd gone apple picking over the weekend, and Jenny couldn't help picturing herself there with Easy, his hands around her waist as she reached for the highest, most perfect red apple she could find and plucked it off the tree. She'd never actually been apple picking before, but it sounded so idyllic. She wondered if they'd ever have the chance to go now. Or if maybe he'd be taking Callie instead. She was so tall he wouldn't even have to help her reach the stupid apple.

"I guess I'm just . . . confused." Jenny stared at the ground. "Why did you want to go out to dinner with Callie?" she finally asked, wondering if Easy could have feelings for both of them at the same time. Maybe, but Jenny wasn't interested in being *one* of the people Easy loved. She wanted to be *the* one.

"It's not that I wanted to." Easy turned to look at her, and she was glad she'd found her sunglasses. "It just seemed easier that way." He leaned down and grabbed a fistful of dry leaves off the ground, then opened his hand and let them float back down to the grass. She waited for him to say more, but he didn't.

It was not the answer she wanted—although she had no idea what answer would have made things all better. Maybe there *wasn't* one. Jenny stared at the brilliant orange oak trees behind Easy, avoiding his eyes. "I don't really know what to say to that. I think I need some time to figure things out." She bit her Stila lip-glossed lip. "Maybe you need to do some figuring out too."

She held her breath, waiting for him to say that he didn't need to figure anything out. That it was *her* he was crazy about, and no amount of thinking would change that. That he was sorry, and that he would be right here waiting for her when she got her own feelings in order. *Say it.*

But Easy just nodded his head slowly, his hands buried deep into the pockets of his faded, paint-splattered Levi's. "'Kay," he half-whispered.

Jenny straightened up. She let out the air she'd been holding in, feeling suddenly . . . deflated. "All right. I'll see you later, then." Her voice came out much colder than she'd meant it to, so she tried to soften it. "Don't miss art class on Friday. You know Mrs. Silver loves you."

Easy smiled. She could see his Adam's apple bobble in his throat. There was a patch of beard scruff beneath his chin that he had missed, and Jenny fought the urge to lean in and kiss him hard, right then and there. Maybe if she had, she could have made things go back to the way they were, before the stupid party, before the stupid dinner, before everything had gotten off track.

But he was already stepping backward, away from her, across the grass. "Right." He touched two fingers of his right hand to his forehead in a mock salute. "I'll . . . uh . . . see you then."

Jenny turned toward the dorms, refusing to look back. What had just happened? Was it . . . over? Tears sprang to her eyes, but she gulped quickly and tried to think happy thoughts: chocolate-sprinkled cupcakes from the Viennese bakery; Barneys sample sales; rainy days curled up inside with an old Nancy Drew mystery; the stately, ivy-covered brick buildings all around her.

But happy thoughts weren't enough to erase the uneasiness she felt. Easy was everything she'd always wanted in a boyfriend—she'd felt so impossibly lucky that he liked *her*. But maybe that was just it. Maybe it *was* impossible.

**OwlNet**

Email Inbox

From: JeremiahMortimer@stlucius.edu
To: BrettMesserschmitt@waverly.edu
Date: Tuesday, October 8, 2:08 P.M.
Subject: Please don't delete

Babe, please answer your phone . . . or let me come see you? I need to explain—I need to talk to you, in person. I'm so, so sorry. What I did was—well, it was the biggest mistake of my life. And for a guy like me, you know that's saying something.

Kidding. But please. Call me.

This is *killing* me. *Please.*

OwlNet

HeathFerro: Hey, sexy. Wanna come over and study for the bio test?

KaraWhalen: Uh . . . I'm not in bio.

HeathFerro: Oh. Well, how 'bout you come over and we find something else to do?

KaraWhalen: That's a gallant offer, but I've got a real study date planned. Some other time.

HeathFerro: You mean it?

KaraWhalen: No.

WAVERLY OWLS KNOW THAT BIRDS OF A FEATHER FLOCK TOGETHER!

"How come the women in here all have enormous boobs?" Brett Messerschmidt asked as she flipped the pages of one of Kara Whalen's *X-Men* comics. She flicked a lock of chin-length fire-engine-red hair out of her eyes. "Is that where they get their superpowers from or something?"

The two girls lay on their stomachs on Brett's silky fuchsia Indian-print comforter, paging through a stack of Kara's comic books. Their chemistry lab had let out early—owing to an "experiment" by the group of geeks who were always huddled together in the library that had ended in a small explosion—and Brett and Kara had planned on using the time to study for their upcoming chem midterm. Their teacher, Mr. Shaw, hated his life and reportedly kept a tally of all the times he had made a student cry, so the test was practically guaranteed to be mind-blowingly impossible. But their study plan had lasted all of three minutes, before Brett flicked on her stereo and asked Kara to bring in some of her vintage comic books. Fortunately, Tinsley had a late-afternoon class on Tuesdays, so they had the room to themselves. Brett had made a point of memorizing Tinsley's schedule and taking advantage of times when her violet-eyed, eternally spiteful roommate wasn't around.

"I don't know," Kara admitted. "Lots of male illustrators, I guess."

"Typical." Brett was still completely bitter about what had happened with Jeremiah. They had been broken up for all of a week and he had managed to actually *sleep* with someone else. To be fair, she was the one who'd broken up with him. But at least she had managed to keep *her* pants on—more or less—and that was more than she could say for *him*. "Guys. All they care about is boobs, boobs, boobs."

She'd already told Jeremiah that it was over for good. A few pleading e-mails had appeared in her inbox, begging her to talk, but she'd deleted them without so much as opening them. If he wanted to stay with her, well, he'd have to find some way to reverse time and undo his hookup with that hippie chick, Elizabeth. Maybe he could look into *that* superpower.

"You should let some of that Jeremiah bitterness out," Kara advised, as if she could read Brett's mind. She wound a lock of stick-straight honey brown hair around her index finger. "Or it's going to eat away at you."

Brett looked up at her in surprise, once again astonished that five days ago she hadn't even known Kara's name. She'd just been the Girl in Black who lived in the room next to the broom closet and was in a couple of her classes. Then, after Tinsley had shown up to Saturday night's party wearing a sexy outfit from Kara's closetful of clothes by her designer mother, Kara had gone from quiet nobody to the cool girl. Cool girl who threw a Waverly mug of warm beer in sleazy Heath Ferro's face, Brett reminded herself. And now here they were: Kara lying on Brett's bed next to her, wearing a flouncy black-and-white polka-dotted skirt and a fitted white button-down, listening to cheesy '80s music and examining bodies of superheroines. What a difference a few days made.

"I can't help it," Brett admitted, twisting her rose-gold stackable rings around her fingers. "I'm just so . . . angry at him."

"You know, when you think about him, your face turns practically the same color as your hair." Kara laughed as she turned over on her back. The corners of her wide-set greenish-brown eyes were accentuated with a teeny touch of Brett's Urban Decay Twice Baked eye shadow. She looked pretty—like she wasn't afraid of people actually noticing her anymore.

"Speaking of which . . ." Brett pulled a lock of her glossy hair in front of her eyes and examined it. It was practically the same shade as her Bourjois Code Red freshly manicured nails. "My roots are showing—I'm way overdue for a coloring. I'm thinking I might go less red this time." When Jacques, her colorist, had first made the mistake and used a blue red instead of a yellow red on her, Brett had been horrified, worried that everyone would start calling her Crayola or Muppet or something. But now she'd gotten used to her somewhat punk-rock coloring, even if it did make her stand out among all her natural-blond and pedigreed-brunette classmates.

"Definitely not." Kara tilted her honey-streaked head, shaking it slowly. "No one at Waverly has hair like you. You look like Jean Grey." She flicked through one of the *X-Men* comics, searching for a picture, and then held it up for Brett to see.

"Oh. When you put it *that* way . . ." Brett laughed. It did make her feel good to think that something made her unique. Not freak-show or trashy-Jersey-girl unique, but rather the-cool-girl-with-the-one-of-a-kind-red-hair unique. She ran her hand over her scalp, tousling her hair to hide the darker roots. "You know, we had a DC meeting over lunch today, and there was this case involving members of the—get this—Competitive Eating club."

"What?" Kara sat up, tossing her head so that her hair fell neatly behind her shoulders. Tiny blondish wisps framed the edges of her face. "What the hell is that?"

"You know. Like, they see how many hot dogs they can eat in ten minutes." Brett sat up too and turned toward Kara. "These two freshmen guys—probably the *only* two members—got caught stealing *four pounds* of raw hot dogs from the dining hall freezer after dinner last week." Kara raised her eyebrows in disbelief. "They defended themselves to the DC by saying they were 'gathering materials for club activities,'" Brett made air quotes with her long fingers, "and that they'd had to resort to covert methods because they hadn't received any funding." She rolled her eyes. "Does the entire male sex suffer from a complete inability to see beyond their carnal impulses?"

Kara leaned back on one elbow and shrugged her petite shoulders. "Well, they *are* freshmen." The comic book slid off the edge of the bed, landing with a slap on the hardwood floor next to Brett's neat piles of notebooks. Brett and Tinsley had moved their beds to opposite sides of Dumbarton 121 when they'd moved in, but that still wasn't far enough.

"Yes, but more important, they're *male*—which means they only think about immediate gratification, with no foresight into the future. I mean, come on—what about Easy?" Brett asked suddenly, sitting up to unbunch the bottoms of her Citizens of Humanity cigarette-leg jeans. "He certainly suffers from the same affliction. I still can't believe he took Callie out to dinner with his dad instead of Jenny."

Kara bit her pink ChapSticked lip. "I saw Jenny last night at the art studio. She just looked so . . . sad." She grabbed her Dasani bottle from on top of Brett's worn oak nightstand and took a long sip. "Do you think she's going to be totally crushed?"

"You mean if Easy and Callie get back together?" Brett shrugged. She honestly didn't know. It was weird. She'd been so used to Easy and Callie as a couple—they'd been practically inseparable all sophomore year—that it was strange to see him suddenly with someone else. But then, to her surprise, she'd quickly gotten used to it. Easy had always seemed a little too . . . nice for Callie. Something about Jenny and Easy together had almost seemed more natural, as if two artistic, like-minded souls had found each other. Not that Brett exactly believed in that romantic crap anymore.

Then again, if Easy was about to dump Jenny, maybe he wasn't as nice as she'd thought.

"Jenny's tougher than she looks," Brett finally answered, surprising herself. She reached up and fingered the gold hoops along the top of her left ear. She was always paranoid about her ears being sort of elfin-shaped, and hoped that the earrings would distract people from noticing.

Kara nodded and sucked in her cheeks like a goldfish, making Brett giggle. "Guys really *do* suck, don't they?"

"Seriously. Why didn't we get the bulletin, like, years ago?" Brett grabbed one of the white goose-down pillows on her bed and started kneading it with her fingers. There wasn't anything especially profound about Kara's statement, but it made Brett's mind start to race. Guys *did* suck, *truly*. Why did she feel like she was the last to know? "If there can be a freaking Waverly club dedicated to the sport of stuffing as much food down the throat as possible, there should be a, like, Guys Suck club—we can let the frosh know before it's too late."

Kara raised her thin, light brown eyebrows skeptically, running a palm over the ridges on the cap to her water bottle.

"Hey, *I'd* join it." Brett put the pillow down emphatically, and it landed on the plush comforter without a sound. Then she hopped off the bed, making her way toward the white iBook on her desk. "Just a place for us to get together and talk and support each other . . ." she went on, the idea taking form in her head. It would be sort of like what Tinsley had originally proposed for her Café Society, although that had immediately dissolved into an excuse to get drunk, do stupid things, and exclude as many people as possible. Brett sat down at her desk. "We could use a little sisterly spirit around here, you know?"

Kara nodded from her perch on the bed. "Actually, I think that's kind of a brilliant idea. Why don't we put together an invite and send it around?"

Brett smiled at her new friend before flipping open her iBook. As much as she hated to admit that she'd do something to spite Tinsley, the idea that she was going to start a club that was more meaningful than Tinsley's shallow, catty, oversexed Café Society gave her an itty-bitty thrill. She felt her green eyes gleaming wickedly as she hit the power button on her laptop. "Agreed. But before we send anything, we need to choose the guest list."

And she knew one roommate who wouldn't be on it.

To: Undisclosed recipients
From: BrettMesserschmidt@waverly.edu
Date: Tuesday, October 8, 3:05 P.M.
Subject: Women of Waverly

Greetings, esteemed classmates.

A couple of us have decided to establish a Women of Waverly club (WoW!) to bolster the sense of sorority on campus. Don't want it to be anything too formal or ritualistic or anything like that (no goats, please), but rather a place for Waverly girls to get together and discuss any issues or concerns facing us on campus. Sex, love, drugs, jerks who call themselves men—anything you want to talk about is fair game.

The first official meeting will be tonight at eight o'clock in the Atrium, and it is open to all female members of the Waverly community. Dining services will be providing snacks and beverages.

Estrogen power,

xo

Brett Messerschmidt

Junior Class Prefect

JulianMcCafferty: Dude, where exactly in Hopkins Hall would I find the Cinephiles screening room? Never been there before.

HeathFerro: Curious request. Before I can hand anything over, I'll need to know why.

JulianMcCafferty: Nothing juicy, Ferro. Just wanted to join up.

HeathFerro: It's in the basement, dipshit.

JulianMcCafferty: Thanks. You're a real sweetheart.

HeathFerro: Kisses.

A SMART OWL WILL TAKE ADVANTAGE OF THE EXTRAORDINARY RESOURCES WAVERLY OFFERS.

Tinsley Carmichael lingered in the screening room in the basement of Hopkins Hall after Signor Giraldi dismissed his Advanced Italian class. They'd just watched Fellini's *La Strada*—much preferable to sitting in a boring old classroom and watching the spit bubble at the corners of Signor Giraldi's mouth as he conjugated Italian verbs. Something about watching old movies, especially old foreign movies, in the dark, leaning back in the leather reclining seats of the screening room, made Tinsley's pulse race. Movie theaters were so freaking sexy. She was ready to tear someone apart. A very specific someone, in fact.

"I can close up, signor," Tinsley purred as the others filed out of the room and Signor Giraldi tried to look like he hadn't just slept through the two-hour film. "I was planning on doing some work for this week's Cinephiles meeting, if you don't mind. I'll be sure to lock the door behind me."

Signor Giraldi glanced at his watch. Rumor had it that he and his wife, who lived in Thompson Hall, one of the girls' dorms, had a standing booty date every afternoon at 3:30 sharp—which was fortunate for his Tuesday afternoon students, as he always let them go a little early. "*Grazie,* Signorina Carmichael." Signor Giraldi smiled absently at her before quickly dashing out the door. Apparently, black-and-white Italian films turned him on too.

The second she was alone, Tinsley dimmed the lights again and propped her Isabella Fiore brown leather stacked-heel boots onto the arm of the chair in front of her. She arranged the hem of her burnt-orange mohair minidress higher on her thigh. With her thick dark hair parted perfectly in the middle and falling in a straight curtain around her face, she felt like an oversexed go-go girl from the '70s. She closed her eyes and waited for Julian.

The soundproof door creaked open behind her. "Hey." Tinsley pressed her eyelids together. Her heart thudded eagerly in her chest. It had been three days since they'd been alone. Last night at dinner, the two of them had sat across from each other at a table filled with their friends, and although Tinsley had been able to feel the weight of Julian's gaze on her face, she'd refused to treat him differently than she did any of the other guys. Which meant that she flirted with him, but only as much as she did with everybody else. The whole situation made her feel like Lily

Bart, the consummate flirt in *The House of Mirth,* a book she'd first picked up when she was thirteen and had read every summer since. She could tell Julian had been a little disappointed, but that was just the way it had to be. She couldn't very well have the entire campus know she was into a freshman.

Tinsley squirmed in her seat. Ten seconds had passed since the door creaked. Was that *not* him? Her eyes flew open.

"Ack!" she squeaked. Julian was standing two feet in front of her, leaning against the back of the chair in front of her, staring down at her face. "Jesus! You scared the shit out of me." Shivers ran down her spine. She hated being surprised—almost as much as she liked it.

"Sorry, m'lady." Julian pulled his left hand from behind his back, revealing a single pink-and-white flower. "For you."

Tinsley politely sniffed at the flower, pretending to be unimpressed. In truth, she loved it when guys brought her things. Last year Bradley Alexander, a senior lacrosse player, had heard about Tinsley's sweet tooth and had tried to woo her with candy, employing other Dumbarton girls to leave packages of Swedish fish outside her door and putting tiny gold boxes of Godiva chocolates in her mailbox every day. It was fun to be showered with attention, but Tinsley could only eat so much candy before she'd start to bloat.

"Thanks," she said, taking Julian's flower and putting it behind her ear.

Julian ran his hands along the tops of the leather chairs but kept his eyes on Tinsley's. He had on a blue pin-striped Abercrombie oxford with the sleeves rolled up to just below his elbows and a

pair of baggy True Religion jeans that were grass-stained at the
knees. "This is awesome. Our own private movie theater."

Tinsley stood up slowly and took a step toward him. She
could feel the heat radiating off his body. "You mean, *my* own
private movie theater," she purred, not touching him. He
smelled slightly sweaty, and Tinsley knew his lips would taste
salty and manly. But she wasn't ready for that yet.

He tried to put his hand on her hip but Tinsley swayed out
of the way. "Sit down. Make yourself comfortable," she ordered
in a sultry voice.

Julian obeyed, sinking backward into the recliner Tinsley
had just vacated. Some boys felt the need to challenge her, but
what she liked about Julian was that he understood her rules.

And she planned on rewarding him for that. Once Julian
was seated, Tinsley carefully perched herself on the right arm
of his chair, stretching her legs across his lap, boot heels tucked
under the left armrest.

"I saw you coming out of Stansfield with Benny today. Those
boots," he said, groaning. He shook his head and traced his finger around the top of one of the boots before slowing running
his hand up to Tinsley's knee, squeezing it gently. She giggled
before slapping his hand away.

Julian pretended to be offended. "Dude, you torture me
with your sexy texts all day, wear this insanely sexy hippie-girl
outfit, drag me down to your secret lair, and now you won't
even let me touch you?" Julian leaned his head back on the set,
his handsome face taking on a pained expression. "You've got
to give me *something*."

"You didn't look very tortured at lunch, when you were chatting up Celine Colista." She slid along the armrest toward Julian until she was practically touching him.

Julian gave a deep, gravelly chuckle. "So is that what this is about? I'm being punished for being friendly?"

She liked that he could tell she was joking. Like she'd ever be worried about someone liking fat-ankled Celine more than her. "That's right. You've been very, very bad."

Julian groaned again as Tinsley traced her long nails around the inside of his collar, clearly enjoying the feel of her fingernails against his neck. She leaned toward him with deliberate slowness, her lips inching toward his a millisecond at a time. When she was about two inches away, close enough to see the tiny golden sparkles in the irises of his eyes, Julian leaned forward abruptly and pressed his lips against her own. A thrill ran through her body—his lips *did* taste salty—and she slid off the armrest and onto his lap.

"I've got to get to practice," she said breathlessly. She wasn't really thinking about practice so much as getting away from Julian. Something about feeling so comfortable with a boy made her a little panicky.

His long arms wrapped themselves around her. "You are *killing* me. I thought we were going to watch a movie—sneak in *Casablanca,* pretend we were stranded in the desert. . . ." He kissed her gently on the collarbone. "I like this spot," he said before kissing it again.

Swiftly, Tinsley extracted herself from his arms and stood up, straightening the hem of her dress. *Deep breaths. He is not*

Humphrey Bogart, and you are not Ingrid Bergman. He is your fresh-man boy toy, and his time is up.

"Do you want to get together tonight at Maxwell? Have coffee? Make out in some dark alcove?" Julian grinned and got to his feet slowly.

"Julian," Tinsley chided, running her fingers through her hair, "we've got to be discreet. We can't just show up at places and make out."

"Well, what if I came to you? In the dark?" Julian started digging through his pockets for something. He pulled out a platinum Zippo with the initials JPM on it and held it out to her. "Take this. After the sun goes down, I'll watch your window. Light it three times, and I'll know it's safe to sneak over."

Tinsley giggled and stared at the lighter in his hand. It was cheesy, sure, but also unbelievably adorable. She grabbed it from his hand.

"Just don't get caught," she warned as she sauntered toward the door.

"I'll wear my cloak of invisibility, promise." Julian put his hand to his heart in a mock pledge.

Tinsley paused in the door frame and opened the lighter, flicking it a few times. She gave Julian her best smoldering look, then turned on her heel and disappeared.

Always leave them wanting more.

 **Owl**Net

BennyCunningham: Juicy alert: saw Mr. Kentucky and Betty Boobs chatting on the quad today, looking less than friendly.

HeathFerro: Guess the honeymoon's o-vah! Think he's back with Georgia peaches?

BennyCunningham: Don't think so. Callie's not one to forgive and forget so quickly. But I'll find out 4sure 2nite at the Women of Waverly meeting.

HeathFerro: WTF's that?

BennyCunningham: Sorry, Heathie. Girls only.

HeathFerro: But that's my favorite kind of club!

WHEN IN DOUBT, A WAVERLY OWL KNOWS TO CONSULT THE TRUSTY RULE HANDBOOK.

Brandon Buchanan grabbed a freshly laundered Lacoste jersey tee from his top dresser drawer and paused before pulling it on to examine his biceps in Heath Ferro's cloudy full-length mirror. He'd been doing more lifting at the gym ever since Julian McCafferty had joined the squash team and he'd found himself having to work a little harder in practice, move a little faster, react a little quicker. He wasn't about to let a frosh take his spot as the star player on the team. For the past two weeks, he'd headed to Lasell after practice and put in an hour or so with the free weights. It was boring as hell, and his muscles ached the next day, but he was pretty sure he was starting to see results.

And he was pretty sure Elizabeth had noticed, too. Elizabeth, the funky St. Lucius girl who'd showed up at the party in Dumbarton trying to track down Jeremiah and had ended up spending all her time with Brandon. Elizabeth, with her pleather jacket and crunchy shoes, who Brandon could absolutely not stop thinking about. At one point on the Saturday night when they were making out in the dark tunnels beneath campus, she had squeezed his bicep and whispered in his ear, her breath warm on his face, "*Nice*." Brandon had assumed she'd been talking about his muscles, anyway, and not his Hugo Boss deodorant, although he might have been mistaken. Elizabeth was one of those girls who seemed insanely unpredictable— even by girl standards.

Which was part of the reason she was so much fun to think about. She wasn't like all the uptight Waverly girls he was used to. He had no idea what she'd be doing right now—was she still in class? Maybe she was back in her dorm room, dancing around to KT Tunstall in her underwear. He'd been pleasantly distracted with thoughts of her ever since she had slipped onto her sea green Vespa and he'd watched her taillights disappear into the darkness as she floored it back to St. Lucius. When he got back to his room, Brandon had been thankful to find that Heath was still out—he'd probably coerced some poor Dumbarton girl to let him sleep in her bed because he "needed to be held." Brandon had been able to fall asleep thinking about the smell of Elizabeth's perfume—something natural and citrusy—instead of the overwhelming scent of Heath's ego.

He'd waited a few days to call her because he knew all too well how easily girls were turned off by the too-eager vibe. But now the waiting was over. He slipped his Bluetooth wireless in his ear and did one last bicep curl in the mirror for luck, but before he could dial Elizabeth's number the door flew open and Heath stormed in, panting.

Brandon quickly stepped away from the mirror, waiting for the inevitable "What were you doing? Making out with yourself?" or "It's not going to get any bigger if you just stare at it in the mirror." But Heath was too distracted to give more than a nod in his direction. He collapsed to his knees next to his own unmade bed, dragging out random shoes and pieces of rancid laundry and tossing them onto the middle of the floor. Brandon eyed the pile he was creating disdainfully. "Finally find a peephole into the girls' showers? Need your camera?"

"I know it's under here somewhere," Heath muttered as he shoved his head and shoulders under the bed and thrashed around for a minute before extracting himself. He halfheartedly tugged at a Louis Vuitton duffel wedged under the bed before immediately giving up. He hopped to his feet, sneezing loudly, his shaggy blond hair covered in dust bunnies, and strode over to Brandon's bookshelf. He tapped his fingers impatiently against his stomach as his eyes scanned each shelf.

"What are you *doing*?" Brandon sighed heavily and turned away. He grabbed his deodorant from his dresser and swiped at his armpits.

"Hardy, Eliot, Hemingway. What do you need so many fucking books for?" Heath sneezed again. *Great. Spread Ferro germs all over.* "Aha!" Heath snatched a black leather-bound book from the third shelf down and Brandon caught a glimpse of gold writing: The Waverly Handbook.

"Looking for new ways to get expelled?" Brandon asked, taking a seat on his navy Nautica comforter.

Heath flopped backward onto his bed and flipped distractedly through the pages of the handbook. "Nah. Hey, you hear about your buddy Walsh yet?" Despite being focused on whatever the secret task was at hand, Heath clearly couldn't resist spreading a little gossip.

Brandon repressed a groan at the sound of Easy's name. "What now?"

"Nothing, apparently." Heath squinted thoughtfully at one of the pages before flicking to another, his right index finger running along the paragraphs, searching for something. "Just heard that Jenny gave him the boot. Callie too. Tired of his shit. Moving on, et cetera, et cetera."

"No shit." That was pretty good news. Even if Brandon *was* pretty much over Callie by now, he still didn't want to see her with slimebag Easy Walsh. And Jenny was waaaaay too good for him too. *Finally* that jackass was getting what he deserved. Maybe there had been some kind of cosmic alignment, the forces of good in the world coming together to keep Walsh from getting away with jerking around two of the prettiest girls on campus. About fucking time. "That true?"

Heath shrugged, still not willing to tear his eyes from the handbook. "That's what my spies tell me."

Brandon pulled his Bluetooth from his ear and tossed it onto his bed. He'd call Elizabeth later, from somewhere private and Ferro-free.

"I knew it!" Heath yelled suddenly, holding up the handbook in triumph. Before Brandon could even ask what he knew, he was running out of the room, waving the book over his head and looking more gleeful than if he *had* found a peephole into the girls' showers.

Sometimes, especially with Heath, it was better not to ask.

A WAVERLY OWL NEVER LIES TO HER PARENTS—
OR HER ROOMMATES.

Callie Vernon hurried home from class on Tuesday afternoon, eager to unload her heavy leather Chloé luggage bag and change out of her Cynthia Rowley pencil skirt. The zipper at the back kept digging into her spine, and Callie was ready to tear it off. She paused for just a moment outside the Pardees' door, where Benny and Rifat Jones and a few other girls were huddled, listening to the fight going on inside.

"They're really going at it," Rifat whispered as Callie approached, pulling a maroon Waverly sweatshirt down over her long, thin torso.

"You just missed some serious name calling," Benny snickered, leaning casually against the wall, already in her practice sweats. "It was great."

It was always fun to listen to the Pardees' fights—all the

other dorms were jealous that Dumbarton got the most volatile faculty couple—but Callie had stuff to do. She raised her eyebrows at Benny and hiked up the stairs.

As Callie opened the door to Dumbarton 303, she paused.

"No, really, Dad, things are going fine here. *Really*," Jenny was insisting into her Treo. Callie stood in the doorway, the heavy tote thumping against her hip, the zipper snagging the delicate fabric of her sateen Diane von Furstenberg jacket. *Damn it*.

Jenny whirled around, her brown eyes opened wide at the sight of Callie. The forced-happy tone in her voice didn't match the sad look in her eyes. For the past few days, she had sort of managed to convince herself that Jenny wasn't really so bothered by the whole Easy thing, after all. Jenny knew that Callie and Easy had gone out to dinner together with Mr. Walsh, but she most certainly did *not* know about their intense closet make-out session, where they had practically inhaled each other. And looking at her sad little roommate, Callie definitely didn't want her to find out.

She started to mouth the words, *Should I go?* but Jenny shook her head vigorously, her mass of dark curls dancing around her pale face, and then turned her attention back to the small black phone held to her ear. "I just . . . wanted to say hi. I've got practice now, so I've got to run, but I'll talk to you later. . . . Love you, too."

Callie flounced into the room, deciding that if she seemed extra cheerful maybe Jenny would catch on and not look so depresso. She dropped her tote crammed with boring

Spanish textbooks onto her bed and tried not to stare at Jenny's puffy-looking eyes. Had she been *crying?* But then Jenny sneezed a cute little rabbit sneeze, and Callie felt a little better, because maybe Jenny was just allergic to autumn or something, and not calling her father for Easy-related solace. "I didn't mean to interrupt your phone call."

Jenny set her Treo down on her dresser and gathered her long hair back behind her head, expertly sliding an elastic from her slim wrist to hold it in place. "No, don't worry about it. My dad just likes me to check in once in a while, or else he starts to think I got, I don't know, inducted into a sorority or something."

"Parents worry way too much." Callie nodded conspiratorially. "Although my parents would probably be thrilled if there were sororities at Waverly." She liked Jenny, she really did, but Easy loomed over them like a storm cloud, and she was pretty sure they could both hear him rumbling in the distance. "It's like they think boarding school is another planet. I know it drives my mother crazy that I'm out of her line of sight when I'm here."

Jenny sighed as she fumbled through a drawer for her practice clothes. "My dad's worried that I'm going to, like, take my first step or something and he won't be there to see it."

"That's sweet." Callie pulled her Ralph Lauren sleeveless mock turtleneck over her head, disappearing for a moment into a tunnel of hair-frizzing static and cashmere. Jenny really *was* just a kid. She was what, fifteen? "My mom worries I'm going to do something to embarrass her, and she won't be there to yell at me for it." She shrugged her shoulders. She could picture Jenny's dad as some super-nice favorite-uncle-type guy who wore chunky hand-knit sweaters and hiking boots and gave the best bear hugs, the kind where you get picked up and spun around. *Her* mom gave her air kisses when she saw her.

Callie strode over to the window seat and turned on her iPod Sound Deck, then twirled the dial when the Donnas came screaming out. Through the thick glass windowpanes, she could see a bunch of girls in soccer uniforms scooping up the fallen leaves and making a giant pile. It looked like fun. It made her think of this time last year, when she and Easy were still new. They couldn't keep their hands off each other and had to sneak to the stables every chance they got just to be alone. She caught a glimpse of her reflection in the glass—in her black Calvin Klein push-up bra, she looked pallid and frail. Not the girl Easy would want to be with.

"I still can't believe she's a governor." Jenny pulled out a bright yellow T-shirt with a giant smiley face on it from her drawer. "I know it's probably a pain but it just sounds so . . . glamorous!"

"It gets old fast." Callie glanced over her shoulder at Jenny, whose back was to her as she struggled to pull her royal blue sports bra down over her massive chest. Callie looked down at her own barely-A's. She'd never really been able to fill out the top of a bikini, but since last year ended, she'd lost some weight, and her breasts had sadly been the first thing to disappear. "Imagine every mistake you ever make becoming, like, public knowledge."

"So, uh . . ." Jenny started, blushing a little as she pulled on a pair of black Adidas gym shorts. She reached up and tightened her ponytail, a few light freckles sprinkled across the pale skin on the underside of her thin arms. "I told Easy today that I kind of needed some time to, you know, figure things out."

"Really?" Callie stared at the bulletin board behind her desk, pretending to check the schedule of field-hockey games thumbtacked to it, unable to look into her roommate's pure, honest eyes. She was proud of herself for telling Easy he had to stop messing around and make his choice—even though she couldn't help wishing he'd just pick her already and get it over with—and wondered what that news meant for her.

"I just . . . feel like I never have any idea what's going through his mind," Jenny admitted, looking a little embarrassed.

"Yeah, no one does." Callie picked up the sweater she'd dropped on the floor and turned to Jenny, tapping a perfectly polished fingernail against her temple. "He's totally messed up."

Jenny giggled and grabbed her field-hockey stick from where she'd stashed it in the corner. "That's one way of putting it." When she glanced back at Callie, a smile was perched on her tiny pink lips.

Callie tossed the sweater onto the floor in front of her closet, where a pile was already building up. The memory of opening that door and finding Easy crouched on the floor in there, hiding, made her heart beat in her ears. Sliding in next to him in the dark, surrounded by her forest of expensive clothes, pulling the door closed, laughing, and then the kissing . . . it had probably been the best moment of Callie's life so far.

She took a deep breath, wondering if maybe Jenny could hear her heart pounding across the room—what was that creepy Edgar Allan Poe story? Where the beating heart of the guy he'd killed ended up getting him busted by the police? Or was it his own guilt that got him in trouble? She should have paid more attention in Miss Rose's lit class.

Callie quickly threw on a pair of black Nike capri pants, a plain white T-shirt, and her maroon Waverly sweatshirt, which was about three sizes too big. Jenny had one sneakered foot balanced on the top of her desk and was bent over her leg, stretching out her hamstring. In her gym shorts and faded gray Berkeley hoodie, her hair pulled back into a high ponytail, she looked cute and sweet, but about as much of a threat as vanilla yogurt.

"Wanna walk over to the fields together?" Callie asked, a little tentatively. Despite having been roommates for over a month now, they'd never once walked to practice together. Callie had always been too . . . *something*. But now she was feeling—what? Generous, maybe? She could afford to be a little kinder to her younger roomie.

After all, one of them was going to get her heart broken—and Callie was pretty sure it wasn't going to be her.

OwlNet

From: beerdude101@hotmail.com
To: HeathFerro@waverly.edu
Date: Tuesday, October 8, 4:13 P.M.
Subject: Your lucky day

Ferro:

Got a bunch of freebie kegs from a microbrewery that's closing up shop and I'm willing to sell them to you at a severe discount.

Act fast—these will not last.

BD

OwlNet

From: HeathFerro@waverly.edu
To: beerdude101@hotmail.com
Date: Tuesday, October 8, 4:16 P.M.
Subject: Re: Your lucky day

Dude—

Sounds tempting, but can't risk having kegs on campus again. Cut it a little close last time . . .

H.F.

From: beerdude101@hotmail.com
To: HeathFerro@waverly.edu
Date: Tuesday, October 8, 4:17 P.M.
Subject: Re: Re: Your lucky day

What about off campus then? My grandma's got a giant barn right
outside town and I wouldn't charge you much to use it. Hay bales, corn
stalks, smell of leaves in the air—and most important, cheap kegs of
beer.

Whaddaya think?

From: HeathFerro@waverly.edu
To: beerdude101@hotmail.com
Date: Tuesday, October 8, 4:19 P.M.
Subject: Re: Re: Re: Your lucky day

Intrigued . . .

6

A WAVERLY OWL SHOULD BE THERE WHEN A
FELLOW OWL REACHES OUT—EVEN IF HE
HATES HIS GUTS.

Easy walked through the woods, his legs sore and tired beneath him after two hours of horseback riding. Whenever Easy had something on his mind, he rode Credo. Something about her enormous brown eyes, looking at him with such unabashed trust, made him feel like he was less of a shit. Because, for the past week, that's how he'd felt. Every single time an image of Callie or Jenny would pop into his brain, he'd think miserably, *I'm an asshole*—which was every other fraction of a second. Credo didn't care if he was an asshole, though. She still stomped her feet happily at the sight of him entering the stables, and she didn't ask him where he'd been or who he'd been with or what he was thinking.

He'd headed to the stables right after talking to Jenny outside the art studio. Not that he'd done much talking—he couldn't find the right thing to say. He couldn't even find the *wrong* thing to say—he simply couldn't think of anything to say. A long, hard ride was exactly what he needed to help him figure his shit out and make up his mind.

The only problem was, it hadn't worked. So instead of having dinner in the dining hall and having eighty people ask him, for the millionth time, if he was with Jenny or Callie, he'd decided to hike to the rocky outcropping in the woods, the one off the boat path, near his secret painting spot. Easy sighed as he settled against a cold, dark rock, pulling a cigar from his pocket. He'd snitched two Cubans from his father's black leather cigar pouch while he'd used the restroom last weekend at Le Petit Coq. It was the perfect occasion to light one and concentrate.

Maybe he should make a list. Like pros and cons? Wasn't that what people did when they couldn't make their minds up between two alternatives? But the idea of breaking Callie and Jenny, two living, breathing girls, down into lists made him want to shoot himself in the foot. Or the head. Okay, maybe not that.

Easy took a giant puff just as he heard a sound out on the path. He held the smoke in his lungs for a long moment, waiting to see if a teacher would appear to get him in trouble. But then a very red-faced Brandon Buchanan materialized, wearing a sweaty white shirt and black running shorts, his vinyl squash bag slung over one shoulder and silver cell phone in hand.

"Sorry, dude," Brandon muttered, running a hand through his sweaty, disheveled hair. He gave Easy a little apology wave with the fingers of one hand and started to turn around.

Easy suddenly realized he didn't really want to be alone. "You don't have to go, man. You can, uh, sit down."

Brandon looked at him for a moment as if it might be a trap, but then he took a step forward and nodded in the direction of Easy's cigar. "Got another?" Whenever Brandon spoke to him, Easy got the feeling he was trying to make his voice sound an octave deeper.

Easy unzipped the front pocket of his black Patagonia vest and pulled out the second Cuban. "It's all yours."

"Light?"

Easy handed him his cheap plastic lighter with the hula girl on it and Brandon nodded at it. "Nice." He lit his cigar and leaned awkwardly back against one of the rocks. He glanced around rapidly, like he still wasn't sure what he was doing here. "So . . ." Brandon inhaled deeply. "How's it been?" he asked through a mouthful of smoke.

Easy sighed and stared at the trails of smoke leading up from their cigars, straight up at the patch of purpley sky visible through the crowd of trees surrounding them. It was more than a little fucked up that he was sitting back smoking stogies with Brandon, the guy whose girlfriend he'd stolen last year—the guy who always looked at him like he wanted to punch him out but never had the balls to do it. "I've been better," Easy replied wryly.

Brandon nodded and propped his sneakers up on another rock. "So I've heard."

Easy stared at Brandon for a moment, trying to judge his capacity for empathy. What the fuck—why not just spill it?

"I'm just . . . all confused," Easy stammered. "I have no fucking clue who I'm supposed to be with." Easy's free hand clenched at his shaggy hair, which was in desperate need of a cut. His father had just about had a coronary when he'd seen it last week.

"You want my opinion?" Brandon asked, his cigar hanging from his weirdly pink lips. He didn't even sound like he wanted to murder Easy, for once. But then, Brandon *had* been all chummy on Saturday night with that mysterious, arty-looking St. Lucius girl—maybe she'd been able to chill him out a little, get him over Callie. Well, good for Brandon. The girl was hot.

"Uh, yeah." Easy held his crappy lighter up to the end of his cigar to relight it. "I guess so."

"All right. Then I'm just going to be honest. I know Jenny is totally sensational and all, but didn't it sort of happen really fast? I mean, she just got here, and suddenly you two were dating." Brandon exhaled smoke straight into the dark evening air. Easy had suspected he'd had a thing for Jenny, too.

"Yeah, I guess it did happen fast." Easy thought back to when he had first really talked to Jenny, that time he'd sneaked into Callie's dorm room and then Callie had disappeared. He'd sat down on Jenny's bed, and everything about her—her smell; her sleepy, makeup-less face; her hair going everywhere; her sweet, curious voice—seemed to be the exact opposite of Callie. "But we just, y'know, hit it off."

"I mean, I get that. Don't get me wrong—I kind of think you're an idiot for not being all completely in love with Jenny. She's just so freaking *cute*." Brandon spoke with the cigar in his mouth, so it was kind of hard to understand, but Easy was catching the drift of it. "But don't you find it a little strange that you went from Callie to, like, the anti-Callie?"

Easy tried to think about why that could be. His mind went immediately back to his ill-fated trip to Barcelona to visit Callie over the summer. A combination of things—the summer in fucking ass-dull Kentucky and his frustration at the thought of yet another full year at suffocating Waverly Academy—had made the trip a nightmare and made Easy dread returning to Waverly even more. And then when he'd gotten back to school, Callie had been even more smothering and bossier than usual, and out of nowhere, this new, cool girl had appeared on the horizon—a perfect way out.

Was that what had happened? Had he used Jenny as a way out of his relationship with Callie because Callie tried to push him too far? Because he wasn't ready to say "I love you"? For the millionth time, he thought of the dinner he'd had with Callie and his father, and how Callie had stood up for him. Memories suddenly flooded his brain—Callie, in her deliciously inappropriate shoes, hiking out to the stables to sneak in an hour of making out before dinner; Callie surprising him with a first edition of William S. Burroughs's *Naked Lunch* for Valentine's Day because she remembered him saying he wanted to read it; Callie, whose hazel eyes made him think of lazy summer days from his childhood and wish he'd known her all his life.

"That's, like, the classic definition of 'on the rebound,' isn't it?" Brandon continued, taking three quick puffs of his cigar and trying to exhale them into smoke rings the way tough guys always do in the movies. "As much as I hate to say it, there was something about you and Callie that just . . . made sense."

Brandon definitely hated to admit it, but it was true. Maybe because Easy and Callie were so clearly *not* suited for each other, they happened to magically be perfectly suited to each other— opposites attract and all that. Didn't make a whole lot of sense, but nothing about love was supposed to.

"Yeah." Easy nodded slowly.

"Go easy on Jenny, you know?" Brandon told him, feeling a little light-headed from the tobacco. Poor Jenny. Brandon could tell from just looking at Easy that he was already dream-ing about Callie and that Jenny didn't stand a chance. Brandon felt a stab of bitterness, but then he suddenly remembered why he had come out here in the first place. Elizabeth. He was over Callie, he was over Jenny. It was Elizabeth all the way.

"Of course." Easy shook his head abruptly as if he had been lost in his daydreams. He glanced at Brandon, his blue eyes suddenly clearer. There was a rumbling in the distance and Easy looked up at the sky, as if it might open up on them, right there and then. "So, uh . . . what about you and that St. Lucius chick?" he asked, toward the clouds overhead.

"Elizabeth." Brandon inhaled deeply, letting the cigar smoke fill his lungs. He was a little proud that Easy had noticed her— of course everyone had, with her funky FREE TIBET T-shirt and long, graceful neck. "Yeah, she's awesome."

Easy nodded. "She seemed cool." He glanced over his shoul-der at the sound of some animal running through the weeds before returning his cigar to his lips.

"She *is* cool." Brandon felt his chest puff out a little with pride, but he tried not to show it. "We had, uh, a really good time . . . hanging out." As much as he was enjoying his cigar, he didn't really want to get all chatty with Easy, at least not about his own shit. "I was just going to call her."

"Call her?" Easy asked, the slightest hint of skepticism in his voice.

Brandon balked. "Why—I shouldn't call her?" he asked, and then hated himself for asking Easy for love advice.

"Nah, I didn't mean that." Easy leaned forward, planting his elbows on his thighs. "Course you should call her. Or write her a poem, do a little sketch, something that shows you've been thinking about her. Be spontaneous." He shrugged.

"Uh, yeah. I'm definitely going to do something." Brandon nodded, sounding more confident than he felt. He was *not* spontaneous by nature. He was the kind of guy who went through the course catalog midsummer and circled the electives he was interested in.

Easy picked a leaf off the ground and crushed it in his palm. He cleared his throat. "Hey. I know it's probably awkward for you to talk me. I know you've always kind of wanted to, like, murder me, but y'know, I'm sorry about . . . all that."

Brandon stubbed his cigar out on one of the rocks and waved it at Easy. "Don't worry about it." They definitely weren't going to be high-fivin' over a keg anytime soon, but still, maybe Easy wasn't a complete prick. "I've got to get back. But thanks for the cigar."

"No problem. Thanks for, uh, hanging out," Easy answered.

"Good luck," Brandon said and meant it, slipping the half-smoked cigar into a pocket of his squash bag. He turned and started back along the path, just as the first drops of rain tickled his new extra-strong arms. Maybe he'd sneak over to St. Lucius tomorrow and surprise Elizabeth in person. That had to be better than some poem or whatever. Right?

A SASSY WAVERLY OWL KNOWS A KISS IS
JUST A KISS.

"Wow. I'd say we got a pretty good turnout." Brett said as Jenny and Kara followed her through the atrium's revolving glass door. The rain outside made a soothing pattering sound against the glass ceiling above them.

The Reynolds Atrium was a two-story space with a glass barrel-vaulted ceiling designed by I.M. Pei, a multimillion-dollar addition to Maxwell Hall completed only a few years ago through the generous support of Ryan Reynolds's contact-lens-billionaire father. The space was filled with leafy ficus trees and ferns, making it feel tropical even in the middle of winter, and when the atrium was lit up, you could see it glowing like a giant lightbulb from across campus. The lobby area was really used only for lame coffee-and-scone get-togethers during Parents' Weekend, and sparsely attended open-mike readings run by *Absinthe,* the Waverly literary magazine. Brett was shocked when she pushed the glass door open and saw dozens of girls crowded around the comfy red Pottery Barn couches, some of them sitting cross-legged on the green-and-gold paisley-pattered carpet.

She felt her stomach start to lurch a little, the way it did before every DC meeting or debate—it was the same sort of queasiness she felt in the seconds leading up to a swan dive into her parents' ginormous kidney-shaped pool. Once she got in the water, so to speak, she was fine. But the jumping made her nervous. Brett wiped her clammy palms against the sides of her dark, skinny-legged Joe's jeans.

The chatter died down as the three girls made their way toward one of the empty red couches near the front of the room that had quite considerately been saved for them. Brett glanced at the girls—almost everyone from Dumbarton was there, minus Tinsley Carmichael, who had been "accidentally" left off the e-mail list.

Brett and Kara sank down onto the couch and watched as Jenny settled onto the floor next to Alison Quentin and . . . Callie? Guess they were friends again. Sort of odd, considering everything they didn't have in common—and the one thing they did. But good for them, getting into the spirit of all this female bonding. Girl power.

"Thank you all for coming," Brett began, trying to make her voice not sound totally authoritative and boring. She was just wearing black leggings and a long navy C&C California tunic, but the girls were all looking at her so expectantly, she might as well have been dressed in her DC formal attire. "Because this is the first meeting of the Women of Waverly, I don't want this to be very formal—I think we should just use this opportunity to get together and talk, and to bring up any issues we have, or any thoughts about what we'd like the club to do in the future." She shrugged her shoulders and glanced around the group as the girls nodded.

Benny Cunningham opened her mouth to say something, but her words were cut off at the sound of the door opening. Suddenly Heath Ferro appeared, wearing a pressed Waverly blazer, his normally unkempt hair combed and plastered into submission. He was waving a book over his head, and to anyone who didn't know him, he looked like a picture-perfect, well-groomed boarding-school boy, eager to learn.

"Don't start without me!" he called out, making his way through the crowd of girls toward the front of the room. Girls giggled but Brett glowered. What the fuck was he doing? When he got close enough to her, he showed her the book he had in his hand—a copy of the Waverly student handbook. "Shall I quote?" he asked, with a self-satisfied smirk on his handsome face. He opened to a page in the handbook and turned around to face the crowd, clearly pleased to be the center of attention. "No Waverly club can exclude members on the basis of sex, gender, or sexual orientation." He slammed the book shut. "Guess that means I'm in."

"I didn't know Waverly offered a law degree," Brett told him snarkily. Heath seemed to have an instinct for showing up exactly where he *wasn't* wanted.

"You looking for a court battle?" Heath smirked back, holding the handbook over his head like a torch.

"Whatever, Heath. That's fine." Brett rolled her eyes and the girls giggled again. "Can you just maybe pretend for a moment not to be such a *guy*?"

"And can you sit down?" Kara asked pointedly. "We were just about to get started."

"No problem, ladies," Heath promised as he patted the pockets of his Abercrombie cargo pants. "But don't we want a group photo first?" He held his tiny silver digital camera up to his face and snapped a picture of the room. He glanced at Brett, who was glaring at him. "Sorry!" he mock-whispered, and slid onto the couch next to Kara.

Brett took a deep breath and tried to forget about the male interloper. "Anyway. In the future we can talk about whatever we want to, but I thought maybe we should start with a topic tonight that can just sort of break the ice." She paused and leaned back on the couch, feeling Heath's eyes on her chest. Perv. Maybe she could shock him right out of the room. "So, how about sex?"

Everyone laughed nervously and looked around, blushing. Brett could tell it would take a little prompting to get things going. "What's your favorite movie sex scene?"

"*Wild Things*," Heath offered immediately, his hand covering his heart in earnest. "Hands down. It's a beautiful piece of cinematic realism," he added, licking his lips.

Brett rolled her eyes. "How about we go around the room?" Brett pointed to Jenny, who was on the opposite side of the circle from Heath.

"Hmm." Jenny rested her chin on her fist. *"Dirty Dancing."* She shrugged her shoulders and looked around the room, her cheeks starting to flush.

"Oh, yeah," Alison agreed.

"What? That's sissy stuff! I mean—"

Brett shot Heath a look that silenced him. "If you're not going to follow the club rules, we'll have to kick you out. *Capice?"*

Heath saluted with two fingers. "Roger, Captain."

"Who's next?" Brett asked, looking over at Callie.

"I'm going to have to go with *Mr. and Mrs. Smith,* Brad Pitt and Angelina Jolie. Definitely." She nodded and turned to Kara, who was on her other side.

"Bound," Kara said. "No contest."

"Now that's what I'm talking about!" Heath cried, pounding a gold swirl of carpet in front of him, an ecstatic look spreading over his face. He held up his hand for Kara to high-five, but she grimaced and looked away.

For the next hour, the girls chatted and laughed about sex. Heath attempted to be respectful the whole time, so much so that all the girls seemed to forget he was there. Brett learned all kinds of things that she never would have guessed about people: that Sage Francis was waiting until marriage to lose it, that Yvonne Stidder was just waiting for college, that Rifat Jones had done it and wished she hadn't. Celine Colista wanted to know if oral sex counted as sex (the vote was divided), and Callie wanted to know if sex really hurt as much as people said. The girls who knew replied sadly that it did, at least the first time. Brett was a little shocked at how open everyone was being about something so personal. But it was such a comfortable, supportive environment that anyone could have said anything and it would have been okay. Brett smiled to herself. Not inviting bitchy, judgmental Tinsley to the group was the smartest decision she'd ever made.

The conversation started to wind down, and some girls got up to refill their mugs with cider or grab another gingerbread cookie. Benny suddenly blurted out, "What I want to know is why guys always assume that if you make out with them, that means you're willing to have sex with them?" she demanded, with an obvious personal investment in the question.

Everyone turned to Heath, as if remembering that he was there. "Wishful thinking." Heath shrugged his shoulders apologetically. "You can't blame us for *trying*."

"Well, that's not really fair," Trisha Reikken spoke up from the edge of one of the red sofas. She was a curvy senior who had a reputation for being willing to do more than kiss. "Why can't guys accept the fact that sometimes a kiss is just a kiss, and that's all they're going get?" She crossed her arms over her ample chest and glared at Heath.

"I hear you." Sage Francis nodded her blond head vigorously. "Guys can get so distracted by the next step, I think sometimes they forget how nice it is to kiss."

"*Some* guys," Heath said pointedly, leaning forward as he spoke. "Me? I love kissing. Kissing is fabulous." He lifted his palms up in an I'm-so-innocent gesture, and everyone laughed. "But, man, so is the next step."

"That's her point, dummy." Kara flicked her index finger

against Heath's shoulder. "Sometimes there *is* no next step. Sometimes kissing is the last stop on the train."

Heath looked like someone had told him there was no Santa Claus. "No next step?" he said, his face ashen. "The next step is why kissing was *invented*!"

All the girls erupted in dissent, angry mumblings running through the group in waves.

Brett raised a hand, calling everyone to order. "I'm sorry, Heath, but I'm going to have to disagree with you there. Some people—people who have the slightest degree of self-control— can appreciate a kiss for what it is, and end it there."

"Right?" Alison nodded emphatically, her silky black hair shiny with the reflection of the atrium's glow. Jenny leaned over to high-five Alison.

"I'm still not sold." Heath shook his head. "You're telling me you can kiss someone and not want more?"

"*I* could." Brett glanced at Kara, who was watching her as she spoke, and a clap of thunder rang out. "I could kiss Kara and appreciate a kiss as being just a kiss." She looked at her friend and shrugged. Maybe this would shut Heath up. Brett brushed her hair back from her face and her lips met Kara's in a quick peck. It was soft and fast and friendly.

"See?" Kara smiled wryly, one eyebrow arching in Heath's direction. "The last stop on the train."

Brett smiled and leaned back against the couch, her head spinning a little. She felt very smug and very . . . warm. The kiss had happened so quickly that she couldn't be sure of anything, but maybe, as her lips had touched Kara's and Brett caught the briefest scent of strawberry lip gloss, she had felt something? Huh . . . that was weird.

Brett grabbed her mug of hot chocolate and tried to follow what the group was talking about now. She glanced over at Heath and noticed that he was staring straight at her, an odd smile on his face. She stuck her tongue out at him and then turned back to the group. The circle had disbanded into smaller conversations, but looking around she could see that most people were only pretending to talk and keeping their eyes on Jenny and Callie, who had turned to face each other at the edge of the circle.

Callie bit her Rosebud-moisturized lips and looked at her roommate's unbearably sweet-looking face. Jenny sat cross-legged on the floor in a pair of charcoal gray yoga pants and a thick oatmeal sweater that she very cutely sort of disappeared in. No matter how much they had competed over Easy, Callie couldn't help but want to hug Jenny right now. Especially after all the feel-good sisterly bonding. She felt like a cheeseball, but it *was* pretty inspiring. "You're an awesome person, and you're my roommate, and I just want us to be friends," Callie finally said, really meaning it. Easy was a Neanderthal. He was *her* Neanderthal, sure, but Jenny was her roommate. And maybe even her friend.

"What if we both just . . . let go of him? For our friendship?" Jenny asked hopefully, her face as sweetly angelic as ever.

Callie's brow unwrinkled and she broke into a wide, relieved smile. It was as if something had clicked in her head. How simple: just let him go and stay friends with her roommate.

She looked again at Jenny's wide-eyed, rosy-cheeked, expectant face. What had Easy Walsh ever done for her, anyway? "That sounds like a plan."

Jenny threw her arms around Callie and Callie patted her back. The roomful of girls gave up pretending not to be listening and burst into applause.

"Now you two! Kiss!" Heath suddenly yelled, pounding the carpet with both hands this time. Once again, everyone had pretty much forgotten he was there. "Kiss! Do it! You know you want—"

Brett picked up a heavy brocade pillow and smacked it into his chest. The meeting was definitely over.

COME HELL OR HIGH WATER, A WAVERLY OWL KEEPS HER PROMISES.

Tinsley poked her head out of her dorm room after a two-hour-long, post-tennis practice nap that stretched all the way through dinner. It was already dark outside and the entire first floor was strangely deserted. The silence was eerie, and it felt almost as though there'd been a nuke scare and she was the only one on campus not hiding in the bomb shelter. What an excellent opportunity to summon Julian. Just the thought of him, sitting across campus, staring out of his Wolcott bedroom window, waiting to catch a glimpse of a little flame, sent shivers down her spine.

Her dorm room window faced the opposite direction, so Tinsley made her way to the bathroom, propping open one of the heavy, opaque glass windows. She flicked on Julian's Zippo, watching the flame shine through the night air once, twice, three times. Her fingers traced Julian's engraved initials.

Not even three minutes had passed—barely enough time for Tinsley to tweeze out some stray eyebrow hairs in the mirror—before she saw an all-black-clad figure veer off the sidewalk and over to the side of Dumbarton. He pressed his back to the brick wall and slowly slid along it, his head darting from side to side as he scoped out the scene.

"Hey," a voice called from below.

"Shh!" Tinsley hissed, sticking her head out the window. Julian reached up and grabbed her hand, anchoring his feet against the brick outside wall and pulling himself up through the window. He stumbled awkwardly to his feet.

"This looks familiar." His eyes darted around the bathroom—no doubt he was remembering that this was the very place they'd first hooked up. "I think I was in here in a dream once," he said jokingly.

"Maybe you were." Tinsley leaned backward against a sink and noticed that Julian was wearing a shell necklace, the kind a girlfriend would buy when she was on vacation in Nantucket or Fire Island. Tinsley, narrowed her eyes. Obviously, she wanted Julian to have had girlfriends before—she didn't want to have to train him completely—but that didn't mean she wanted to see remnants of them hanging off him.

"Nah, it couldn't have been a dream." He glanced over his shoulder at Tinsley and his dark eyes called her toward him. She wanted him to come to *her,* but she couldn't resist. "You always wake up from them."

Tinsley stepped away from the sink, her bare feet touching the cold tile floor of the shower. She pulled the curtain closed

behind her and ran one hand across Julian's chest. She pushed
him against the stall wall and kissed him like she hadn't seen
him in months, though in reality it had been about three hours.

"Did you miss me?" she teased, in between kisses. His hands
were gripping her sides, his fingers playing with the bottom of
her red American Apparel T-shirt, begging to be allowed to go
underneath.

Julian growled and his hands touched Tinsley's bare skin.
She shuddered a little, as they crept oh-so-slowly up her ribs,
and just as she was about to slap them away—he couldn't go
there without asking permission, of course—the bathroom door
rattled open with a loud clang. They pulled their lips apart and
their eyes widened in surprise, but Julian didn't take his hands
off of Tinsley's body.

Tinsley pressed a finger to Julian's lips, her pulse racing.
As they held their breath the intruder started to sing, "Da de
da de da dum . . . da de da de da dum . . ." Julian's beautiful
eyes formed question marks as Tinsley tried to determine the
person who belonged to that voice. It wouldn't be a big deal
if it was a girl who was easy to push over, like a sophomore or
a nerd—Tinsley could just enlist the girl's help in sneaking
Julian into her room, and they could continue their romantic
interlude there. The two of them tried not to giggle as they
listened to the sounds of peeing. Just as she was about to peek
around the curtain, the voice broke into words: "Don't stand,
don't stand so, don't stand so close to me. . . ."

Tinsley's jaw dropped. *Fuck.* Of course Pardee was a cheesy
Police fan. Tinsley had heard—the whole first floor had heard—

the dorm adviser, Angelica Pardee, complaining loudly to her husband this morning to either fix their shower or find "a real man" who could. Apparently, he'd been unable to do so. Tinsley pressed her finger harder against Julian's lips as they heard her flip-flops slapping against the hard floors. How was she going to spin this one if Pardee pulled back the curtain and found Tinsley in the shower stall with a guy?

Then came the sound of the curtain of the adjacent stall being pulled back and the water being turned on. Jesus. That was close. "Come on," she mouthed, nodding toward the door. "We've got to get you out of here."

Julian feigned not understanding, and whispered back at her, "What? You want to make out some more?" He leaned in to kiss her.

"Later!" she accidentally said out loud, thankfully at the same moment that Pardee broke into song once again.

"*Her friends are so jealous, you know how bad girls get. . . .*"

Tinsley rolled her eyes, inching back the shower curtain and sneaking through, pulling Julian behind her. She motioned toward the window, but just as he was about to step through it, a group of girls appeared on the sidewalk, heading toward the dorm's front entrance. Damn it. There was no way Tinsley could let them see her sneak Julian out of the bathroom window—it would take about five seconds before the entire campus knew that she was hooking up with a freaking freshman.

"Not that way," Tinsley whispered urgently. She tugged him away from the window, almost making him fall, then dragged him, tiptoeing, out the door. He tried to kiss her again but

Tinsley slapped him away, a little more violently than she'd intended to.

"You can sneak out my window," she hissed. But before they were halfway down the hall, the front door started to open, and she quickly grabbed the handle of the broom closet, stuffing a protesting Julian inside.

"What are you doing?" His muffled voice came from inside the closet as a cluster of giggling girls turned down the corridor.

"I'll get you in a minute, when it's safe," Tinsley growled under her breath. She quickly removed the irritated look from her face and strode toward her room, trying to look as natural as possible.

"T!" Sage Francis cried out just as Tinsley had reached the door to her bedroom. "Where the hell were you?"

Tinsley looked from her to the other girls, not comprehending. "What are you talking about?" she asked with icy disinterest, her hand poised on her doorknob.

"You missed the Women of Waverly meeting?" Sage shook her corn-silk-blond hair back and forth, chewing a wad of bubble gum too big for her mouth. Sage had recently read something online about how an hour of gum-chewing burned a hundred calories, and she had quickly adopted the habit, dying to shed the five pounds that were always plaguing her. But Tinsley thought the overpowering scent of spearmint had to be doing Sage's love life more harm than good.

"The what?" Tinsley didn't know what she was talking about, and she didn't much care. So long as nobody knew what she'd been doing for the last half hour.

Sage's jaw dropped. "Did you *not* get Brett's e-mail?" Her eyebrows were raised in concern, but she clearly loved knowing something Tinsley didn't.

"The . . . uh, Women of Waverly?" Tinsley made her voice as disdainful as possible. The *Women of Waverly?* It bored her just to *say* it.

"Well, you missed out!" Sage's voice was bubbling over with excitement, and Tinsley couldn't help feeling a twinge of jealousy that everyone had done something she hadn't. Sage tugged at something underneath her thick navy turtleneck. "Sorry, this underwire keeps, like, stabbing me."

Tinsley simply raised a dark, neatly plucked eyebrow, trying not to be annoyed. She fingered the doorknob, part of her wanting to slam the door in Sage's smug face and leave her there adjusting her bra, part of her wanting to know what Sage was talking about. She'd be damned if she'd ask another question about Brett's stupid club, but still, that didn't mean she didn't want to *hear* about it.

Sage finally glanced up and saw Tinsley's irritated look. "Sorry," she said quickly. "I've got to change. But come up with me—I'll fill you in."

"Sure, whatever." Tinsley stalked up the stairs, following Sage as she prattled on, leaving a trail of yellow and orange leaves from the bottom of her magenta-and-lime plaid Burberry wellies as she walked. Tinsley was so caught up in how not jealous she was feeling that she'd forgotten all about what she'd been doing that night—and that Julian was in a dark broom closet, wondering what the hell was taking her so long.

EasyWalsh: What're you doing? I need to talk to you.

CallieVernon: 'Bout what?

EasyWalsh: In person. Could you sneak out? Meet me at the stables tonight?

CallieVernon: Tonite? I'm busy.

EasyWalsh: Please? It's important.

CallieVernon: If you want to talk to me so badly, you're just going to have to wait until tomorrow. In the daylight.

EasyWalsh: All right. Before bio lab?

CallieVernon: Whatever. I've got some news for you too.

EasyWalsh: 'Kay. Miss you. G'night.

CallieVernon has signed off.

OwlNet

JulianMcCafferty: Dude, did you relock the tunnels on your way back home last weekend?

HeathFerro: Whaddya mean? The door in Lasell?

JulianMcCafferty: In Dumbarton.

HeathFerro: UR shit outta luck—locked it behind us. Didn't want any strangers sneaking in.

JulianMcCafferty: U know any other ways out?

HeathFerro: WTF R U doing over there now? Tinsley give you a booty call?

JulianMcCafferty: You're such an idiot.

HeathFerro: Listen, bro, if you've figured out how to get into her pants, you can definitely figure out how to get out of that dorm.

WAVERLY OWLS DO NOT SNEAK INTO OPPOSITE-SEX DORMS—UNLESS THEY HAVE A WAY OUT.

Jenny walked carefully over toward Callie, trying not to spill the mugs of hot cider she held in either hand. Her roommate was perched on the edge of one of the red couches, holding her cell and texting furiously. After the Women of Waverly meeting officially disbanded ten minutes earlier, Brett and Kara had been attacked by swarms of happy girls wanting to thank them for putting the whole thing together, leaving Jenny and Callie on their own. As she approached with the mugs, she saw Callie drop her phone back into the pocket of her navy Ralph Lauren raincoat.

"Thanks," Callie said, looking up with surprise as Jenny handed her the mug. Her cheeks were flushed, and Jenny couldn't help but wonder if it was due to the sweltering temperature inside the atrium or whatever she'd just been texting about.

"Wanna head back?" Jenny asked, putting down her cider as she realized she was too hot to drink it. Even though she'd taken off her heavy wool sweater and was just wearing a thin black Club Monaco tee, she could feel that her bra was damp with sweat. Gross.

"Yes," Callie answered, looking relieved. "Let's go." The two of them headed out into the dark, chilly night, and Jenny stopped for a minute, letting the cool air hit her hot skin before pulling on her sweater. Up ahead of them a flock of other girls made their way back to the dorms. Callie and Jenny lagged behind a little, the only noise coming from the dried leaves crunching under their shoes. They weren't talking, but for the first time Jenny could tell that it was a comfortable silence that had fallen between them.

In some ways it was sad that things with Easy were officially over, that she'd made a pact with Callie, and that now even if Easy came back and said he loved her, she'd have to refuse him. But looking into Callie's eyes and promising in front of the whole world that their friendship would always come before Easy, or any other boy for that matter, made Jenny realize how crippled with guilt she'd been over the whole situation. Maybe if she were a different person, someone like Tinsley, she could have dated Easy without the guilt, and it could have been wonderful. But she was done with trying to be someone else. She was Jenny Humphrey, like it or not, and Jenny Humphrey did not steal other people's boyfriends.

"Hey, I'm going to leave a note for Brett," Jenny said as they stepped into the lobby of Dumbarton. The floor was covered with leaves and dozens of girls' footprints. Pardee was going to be pissed tomorrow when she saw the mess.

"'Kay." Callie grinned at Jenny over her shoulder as she walked toward the staircase. Jenny watched her for a second. Despite the fact that Callie had tightened the drawstring on her gray flannel L.A.M.B. pants as much as humanly possible, the pants still sagged down to her hips, revealing a tiny strawberry-shaped birthmark near her bony spine. Jenny wished she could stuff some cookies into her, but even the delicious, warm gingerbread ones hadn't tempted Callie at the meeting tonight. "See you later, roomie!" She waved as she disappeared from sight.

Jenny smiled back at her, still feeling all warm and fuzzy from the meeting, and headed toward Brett's room. As she passed the hall broom closet she paused. What was that beeping sound? It was faint, but it was definitely coming from the closet. Curious, Jenny cracked open the door.

"Ohmigod!" She jumped back. There was someone in there! A *guy*! She might have screamed if she hadn't quickly recognized Julian, that tall freshman who was always hanging out with the older boys. He was holding a black cell phone in his right hand, his thumb poised to start texting.

"Shhh!" he hissed, looking almost as startled as she felt.

"What are you *doing* here?" Jenny whispered back, glancing down the hallway. She couldn't see anyone, but she could hear Benny Cunningham and some other girls in the lounge watching *Grey's Anatomy* reruns.

"I was, uh . . ." Julian's pupils were dilated from standing

in the dark, making Jenny wonder how long he'd been in the
closet. And how he got there in the first place. "Looking for
something I left here this weekend."

Jenny smiled skeptically. "What, your cleaning supplies?"
She leaned her head against the edge of the door, suddenly very
conscious of the presence of a boy in Dumbarton.

Julian toyed with the frayed edge of his tight-fitting Pearl
Jam T-shirt. A charcoal gray flannel shirt was tied carelessly
around his waist. "Well, leave no stone unturned, and all
that."

"Oh, sure." Jenny raised her eyebrows and played along,
wishing she was wearing something more exciting than her
chunky wool Diesel sweater. "So, uh, what exactly is it you're
looking for?"

His brown eyes gleamed in the darkness, as if her question
surprised him. Jenny couldn't help giggling. It was kind of
fun to watch him struggle. He peered over Jenny's shoulder.
"My . . . uh . . . my lighter."

Jenny nodded sympathetically and tapped her nails against
the cool brass doorknob. "I'll keep my eyes open for it. What's
it look like?"

"A Zippo. Silver, my initials—JPM—engraved on it." He
paused and grinned, revealing a tiny dimple below his slightly
chapped lips. "Have you seen it?"

"Sorry." Jenny giggled and shook her head, conscious of how
frizzy her hair probably looked right now. "What's the *P* stand
for?"

Julian unwrapped his shirt from his waist and stuck his arms into it but left it unbuttoned. His head bumped against the empty shelf at the top of the closet—he was tall. "Padgett."

"Padgett," she repeated, nodding thoughtfully. Must be one of those family names. "That's cool."

"Look, don't get me wrong," Julian started, scratching his head. "I'm having a good time talking to you and all, but, um, I'm not too crazy about the idea of getting expelled. And you probably don't want people to think you're crazy, talking to a broom closet."

"Oh, right." She giggled. "Let me go do some surveillance." Jenny closed the door softly and crept down the hall to the lounge. About eight girls were glued to the television, and they weren't going to move until their show was over, not even for commercials. She whirled around and almost ran straight into Angelica Pardee as she came out of the bathroom in a thick, flowered robe that looked like something from her grandmother's closet, her hair wound up tightly into a white towel turban. "Hi!" Jenny said brightly, stepping to the side to let her pass.

"Hi, Jenny." Pardee nodded, her characteristic look of annoyance spread across her damp face. "Have you noticed that there seems to be low flow in those shower heads?"

"No, uh, I hadn't." Jenny tried to keep her voice sounding normal, but she could tell from the way Pardee was looking at her that she must sound funny. She'd never won at a game of poker in her life.

"All right." Pardee sighed and headed back toward her apartment at the end of the hall. "I guess I'll have to talk to buildings and grounds about that too." Her flip-flops thwacked against the polished mahogany wood floor, leaving a trail of wet footprints in her wake. At least she hadn't noticed the muddy leaves. Jenny waited until she heard Pardee's door lock before she threw open the closet door.

"Quick! Pardee's getting dressed right now, so it's the perfect chance."

"You're sure it's safe?" Julian asked nervously, peeking out into the hallway. "I'm kind of getting used to it in here."

Jenny giggled again and grabbed his arm, tugging him down the hall. Her heart raced and she felt like she was playing hide-and-seek. "Just stop talking!" she whispered, slowing down when they approached Pardee's door. The two of them tiptoed past it, then toward the back door. Jenny didn't breathe again until the door was open, and Julian was standing on the grass outside.

"There," she whispered firmly. "Now, get out of here!" She tried to sound stern but a smile crept into her voice.

Julian exaggeratedly wiped the back of his hand across his forehead. "My guardian angel. You saved my life."

"Fine. You owe me one." Jenny made a shooing gesture with her hands. "I'll keep looking for your lighter, Padgett."

Julian gave her a funny smile that she couldn't really decipher. "See you around," he said finally, and then disappeared into the moonless night.

Jenny stood in the doorway by herself for a moment, taking a deep breath of autumn air before bursting into laughter. Her relationship with Easy might be on its last gasp, but suddenly it seemed other boys might breathe some life into Waverly too.

OwlNet   Instant Message Inbox

JulianMcCafferty: Hey, where'd you go?

TinsleyCarmichael: Ohmigod, are you out? I forgot all about you.

JulianMcCafferty: I kind of noticed.

TinsleyCarmichael: Sorry 'bout that—something came up. I'll make it up to you.

JulianMcCafferty: Yeah? How?

TinsleyCarmichael: I'll see you tomorrow. We can finish what we started.

JulianMcCafferty: Think about the ways in which you can apologize.

TinsleyCarmichael: I'm thinking. . . .

PRIVATE OWL CONVERSATIONS SHOULD HAPPEN
PRIVATELY. AS IN, NOT IN PUBLIC.

Unbearably early the next morning, Callie stood in the doorway of her Latin class, willing herself not to fall asleep on her Chloé knee-high-booted feet. The only way she could manage to get out of bed on Monday and Wednesday mornings was to set out a new outfit the night before. Today she wore her Iisli cashmere wrap sweater in the palest pink imaginable, a brand-new Theory black skirt with a kick pleat in the front, a sexy pair of hand-crocheted black tights, and her black leather riding boots. But neither her sexy outfit nor the adrenaline high from last night's girl-talk meeting could keep her spirits up—Latin was mind-bendingly boring, and Mr. Gaston, who, every Wednesday called on one student to recite five lines of the *Aeneid* from *memory,* did not make it any more bearable. She paused outside the door to his classroom to take five deep breaths.

"Can we talk for a sec?" Easy suddenly stood in front of her, wearing his army-green-and-gold-striped wool sweater— the one with the holes in the elbows. Callie hated that she knew every piece of his wardrobe by heart. And that she had his schedule memorized and therefore knew when she could and couldn't expect to see him. He was supposed to be across campus right now, in Webster Hall. So what was he doing *here?*

"What's up?" Callie tried to make her voice sound apathetic, but she couldn't help it—the moment she laid eyes on him, she trembled a little. She tried to think about Mr. Gaston calling on her to recite a passage from Ovid and that calmed her a bit—but also soured her mood. "I *told* you we could talk before bio."

Easy placed his hand on Callie's arm and pulled her to the corner of the hallway, out of the way of people entering the classroom, and stared at them knowingly. "I couldn't wait that long. Look, I . . ." His voice trailed off. He did look kind of awful, like he hadn't been able to sleep last night. But chances were, it wasn't because he was thinking about her or anything—he was probably just playing stupid video games until 3 A.M. again. She steeled herself against him. "I want to get back together."

With me? Or with Jenny? Callie couldn't help thinking. She stared at the dark circles under his eyes and wound the soft pink sash of her sweater around her fist. "Wh . . . what?" She looked up just as Benny Cunningham, in an unflattering kelly-green-and-navy-striped polo dress—um, hello, *horizontal stripes?*—

stepped into the classroom, but not before giving Callie a giant, totally obvious wink.

"I made a huge mistake." Easy's dark blue eyes looked sadder than she'd ever seen them. He was wearing a pair of Levi's that were begging to be thrown into the garbage, and he had a splotch of toothpaste at the corner of his lips. "I really didn't mean to hurt you. I think I just needed some, um, time to think." He gulped. "But I love you," he blurted out, as though he'd said it a million times before.

Callie bit the inside of her cheek, her heart aching in her chest. She'd wanted Easy to love her for practically ever. Okay, well, for months, and it had *felt* like forever. But his timing could not have been worse. Last night, in front of practically the entire school, she and Jenny had made a pact to put their friendship before Easy. Why couldn't Easy have said this to her *yesterday*?

"So you broke up with Jenny?" Callie asked suddenly, remembering that last she'd heard—from Jenny—*she'd* been the one to suggest they take a little time to think.

Easy stared down at his shoes. The worn-out toes of his brown Vans looked funny against the freshly polished marble of the hallway floor. "Yeah, well, I haven't actually done that yet."

"You've made everything much too complicated." Callie couldn't look into Easy's eyes—it was too hard. She was afraid he'd be able to see through all her bravado and realize how much she missed him, and how much she longed to just lean into his arms and pretend it was last year. But it *wasn't*, and

Easy couldn't make it all go away by just snapping his fingers. "Just because you feel this way now doesn't mean you'll feel this way tomorrow. How am I supposed to know that you're not going to just change your mind *again*?"

Callie looked down and suddenly remembered that her Chloé kitten-heel riding boots were the same ones she'd been wearing that awful day when Easy told her it was over. When she'd had to cross the quad, bawling, in front of the entire world, to go back to her room and hide and cry on Tinsley's shoulder, feeling like her life was over. That had been the worst day of her life—and she'd had some bad ones, like when she'd broken her collarbone falling off a horse and her kitten, Butterscotch, had been hit by a car on the same exact day. But nothing had compared to how completely rejected she'd felt when Easy had dumped her like that, so heartlessly and out of the blue.

Easy opened his mouth to say something, but Callie cut him off, tapping the toe of her boot against the hard marble floor. "*No.*" She liked the way the sound of her voice resonated in the now-quiet hallway—it made her feel tough. "We can be friends. That's it. You can't always get what you want, Easy Walsh, whenever you want it."

She hadn't realized how much she'd let her anger creep into her voice until Mr. Gaston appeared in the doorway of his classroom, his black mustache twitching with irritation. "Is everything all right here?"

"Yes, we were just finishing up a conversation." Callie nodded firmly and, with a last look over her shoulder, slid past Mr. Gaston into the classroom, leaving Easy alone in the empty hallway.

She was glad she'd told him off and gotten the final say. Except she couldn't quite help thinking about how nice those words—those three gorgeous words—had sounded coming from his mouth.

IT IS COMMON COURTESY FOR A WAVERLY OWL TO SHARE THE CONTENTS OF A CARE PACKAGE WITH FELLOW OWLS.

At noon, the mailroom in Maxwell Hall was pulsing with life as the Waverly Owls scrambled to check their mailboxes before lunch, hoping to find love letters, the new issue of *W,* or, better than all else, a *package slip.* Tinsley had to stand on her tiptoes to see into Box 270, on the top row. One would have thought the administration would have enough sense to give the highest mailboxes to the basketball giants and the lower ones to Waverly's less vertical. Normally, Tinsley didn't mind the stretch—she knew she looked kind of sexy standing on her toes, her sweater rising to reveal some skin—but today she happened to be wearing her Miu Miu red velvet skimmers that were as flat as flat could be, with a short black cord Free People frock dress. The dress was sure to flash her behind if she tried to stretch too far. While Tinsley wasn't exactly modest, she wasn't about to give the entire mailroom a free show, either. Frustrated, she hopped up, trying to peek into the slot, her heavy leather Juicy messenger bag thumping awkwardly against her hip.

"Having trouble?" a voice piped behind her. "I bet you're just praying for someone really tall . . . and handsome . . . and *young* . . . to come along and help you."

Tinsley rolled her eyes at the sound of Heath Ferro's voice, turning to face him. He was wearing a pale yellow Lacoste polo that looked blindingly new, the collar turned up. He looked like he should be golfing.

"Do you mind?" she asked, faux sweetly, determined not to let her irritation show. Was that supposed to be some sort of crack about Julian? "Can you grab the mail from my box, or is that too much to ask from a superhero?"

"I could never refuse a damsel in distress," Heath said gallantly, effortlessly reaching his hand into her mailbox. "'Cept you have to promise to share." He held out a coveted yellow PACKAGE TOO LARGE FOR BOX slip over Tinsley's head.

She laughed and rested one hand on her hip, not about to jump through hoops for Heath Ferro. "Oh, I'm sure it's nothing you'd be interested in. Probably just the new La Perla panties I ordered."

"You definitely have to share, then." Heath pretended to faint as Tinsley snatched the slip from his hand. "I thought girls didn't say 'panties,' though?"

"They do when guys are around." Tinsley made a beeline for the mailroom pickup window, Heath following like a puppy dog. Didn't he have anything better to do? "Two seventy," she said, handing the girl behind the counter her slip. She was quickly rewarded with a shoe-box-size package.

"Adea, huh?" Heath asked, leaning over her shoulder to look.

"How'd you—oh." Tinsley looked down at the package, realizing her mother had included her middle name in the address: Tinsley Adea Carmichael. "It was my Danish grandmother's name," she mumbled, the rest of the address catching her eye. In her mother's elegant backwards-slanting cursive, it was marked to Box 207. Jesus, this was her third year here, and her mother *still* didn't have the right address. This had better be something good. The return address was her parents' Gramercy Park penthouse. Hmm. She'd thought they were in Amsterdam—her father was orchestrating some fancy business deal—but of course they hadn't kept her up to speed on their plans.

"I'll buy you a mochaccino if you show me what's in the box," Heath bargained as Tinsley slid the package under her arm.

"It's your lucky day, Ferro." She shrugged, and the two of them headed toward the coffee bar. She always needed a little pick-me-up around this time, or else she found it impossible to make it through her afternoon classes.

"So, Julian, huh?" Heath glanced at Tinsley out of the corner of his eye, a perfectly angelic expression on his handsome features. The two of them carefully stepped over an abandoned J.Crew catalog as they made their way out of the mailroom.

Bastard. He definitely knew something. And if Heath knew about it, then the entire campus wasn't far behind. She quickly put her hand on his forearm and gave it a squeeze, lowering her voice to the throaty register she knew made boys think about sex, and nothing else. "You know *you're* the only one for me, H.F."

"Ha!" He pretended to eye Tinsley suspiciously but she could see that gooey look come into his eyes. Heath was so horny that a little dose of the signature Carmichael charm was all that was needed to make him forget about Julian. For now. "You're such a tease," he said, holding open the door to the coffee bar and following her as she made her way toward the line. He ordered and paid, and Tinsley went to pick up the drinks from the barista.

"So, get this." Heath followed her as she strode over to a booth in the corner. She dropped her box onto the table disinterestedly and slid onto one padded red-leather bench. Heath glanced around him—like that wasn't suspicious—before continuing in a hushed voice. "My connection at the liquor store says he can get us some killer cheap kegs and even offered up his family's barn somewhere in town." He stretched his arms into the air so that his shirt rose to reveal his tanned, tight abs. "Think there's any way we could bribe Marymount to let us all go off campus?"

Tinsley raised her eyebrows and dug into her purse. She pulled out the miniature Sephora nail file she kept with her at all times, prying the tape off the package from her mother. Not only did the nail file come in handy for manicure-related emergencies, it made her feel like Nancy Drew. Or MacGyver. "What if *I* bring the idea to him?" The wheels were already turning—Marymount definitely owed her for keeping his secrets to herself. The Boston weekend had been weeks ago, and she and Heath and Callie had all managed—somewhat amazingly—to keep mum about catching him canoodling with the equally married Angelica Pardee. Now it was *definitely* Marymount's turn to thank her for it.

"Sweetheart, you're pretty, but you're not that pretty." Heath grabbed for the package, but Tinsley pulled it away from him. "You think if you ask him to let you have a keg party off campus and show him a little leg, he'll say yes?"

"No, dipshit." Tinsley peeked into the package, glimpsing the shimmery gold box with the word *Teuscher* on it. Mmm. Swiss truffles. These were definitely for sharing. She pulled out the box, opened it slightly, and removed the five crisp one-hundred-dollar bills that were neatly placed on top of the padding inside. Her mom always sent her cash, as if she didn't have an ATM card—and as if there were anything in Rhinecliff to spend money on besides tie-dye shirts and weed. Still, it was a sweet gesture. "I'd be a little more creative than that. Spin it as something more legitimate . . . like a Cinefiles outdoor screening." She was impressed with her own quick thinking. She really *was* like Nancy Drew, with a naughty streak.

Heath pounced on the chocolates, stuffing two in his mouth at once. Tinsley stared at him, a little impressed that he could simultaneously be so gross and still so handsome. "Think that'll work?" he asked through a mouthful of praline.

Tinsley plucked a double-chocolate raspberry truffle from its delicate tissue bed and placed it on her tongue, allowing the luxurious flavors to slowly melt into her mouth. She leaned her head back against the booth and closed her eyes. Only when the round chocolate had completely disappeared could she be bothered to open a single violet-colored eye to respond.

"I *know* it will."

A WAVERLY OWL KNOWS ALL GOOD THINGS MUST
COME TO AN END—AND THAT SOMETIMES IT'S
BETTER THAT WAY.

"Your *homework*," Mrs. Silver announced Wednesday afternoon, emphasizing the word *homework* even though Jenny knew that no one in their human-figure drawing elective thought of it as that, "will be to do a drawing or painting of a member of the opposite sex that attempts to reveal something about their personality." Her Mrs. Claus–blue eyes twinkled. "Be creative. And please bring them in on Friday." She raised her voice to carry over the noises of her students flipping their sketch pads closed and tossing their pencils back into their boxes. "Some prospectives will be visiting campus this weekend, and I'd like them to see how talented our art students are."

Jenny plunked her thick piece of charcoal back into a special compartment in her ArtBin pencil box and tried not to think about the day that Easy had asked her to meet him at his special clearing in the woods and taken her portrait. Everything about that day seemed perfect now, and Jenny wished she could somehow freeze that memory and remember it without all the yucky, complicated stuff that came along with it.

Right now, Easy was all the way across the room, on a stool next to Parker DuBois, taking notes in his Moleskine sketchbook. She was serious about the pact she'd made with Callie—although, from the way Easy was acting, maybe it wasn't even necessary. Maybe Easy was already over her.

"Oh, and children—I'd like you to branch out and use someone outside this class as your model." Mrs. Silver twitched her round little nose. "Shake things up a bit." She shook her hips like a hula dancer, as if to illustrate what she meant.

Jenny immediately felt relieved. Good. Now she and Easy would definitely not be able to draw each other. So she didn't have to worry about him saying no.

Even though she'd been thinking all morning about how she was going to have to break up with him—if they were even still going out, which she wasn't sure they were—she really didn't feel like doing it today. Not when she was wearing her favorite Citizens of Humanity jeans that had been a Christmas present from her father and represented the single time he'd bought her an article of clothing that she would actually wear in public. Sure, she'd e-mailed him a picture of the exact pair she wanted from Saks.com, size and everything, but she hadn't expected him to actually *buy* them for her. She didn't want them to become the jeans she was wearing when her relationship with Easy ended.

"Do you want to get a cup of coffee before practice?" Jenny asked Kara as they washed the charcoal off their hands at the sinks in the back of the studio. She knew it was neurotic, but she just didn't want to be alone right now. Alison had already snuck out of class early to meet up with Alan for a Latin study date in the library—even *that* sounded good to Jenny.

"I'm sorry, I can't." Kara dried her hands off on one of the stiff brown industrial-quality paper towels they always seemed to have in art buildings. "I've got a meeting with Mr. Wilde to talk about my history paper."

"Oh." Jenny smiled at her friend. "Lucky you." She was already looking forward to AP American History next year. She'd passed the super-cute Mr. Wilde in Stansfield Hall once and had seen that he was wearing a Modest Mouse T-shirt underneath his neatly pressed blue button-down and tie.

The girls picked up their bags and walked down the hallway and out of the building. Jenny glanced around but didn't see Easy anywhere. Kara pulled a tube of cherry Blistex from the pocket of her worn-out jean jacket and spread it across her lips. "Well, let's just say history is the one class I never mind getting help in." She winked at Jenny as they pushed open the double doors to the outside world and warm sunshine beamed down on them, the entire campus painted in brightly colored reds and oranges and yellows before them.

Jenny waved goodbye to Kara and watched her friend walk off. She paused to pull her aviators out from her bag and saw that there, leaning against one of the columns, was Easy Walsh, waiting for her.

"Can I walk with you?" Easy shielded his eyes from the sun with one hand while the other held his sketchbook. Jenny shifted her heavy bag to her other shoulder.

"Sure." The two of them quietly fell in step together, cutting across the quad. Giant oak leaves were scattered across the grass, and Jenny bent over to pick one up. It was yellow with orange spots, and so pretty Jenny thought she'd like to press it between wax paper and give it to her dad. Maybe make a bookmark out of that. Hadn't she done that once, at art camp? She tried to think about this new project—or really, anything other than what Easy was about to say.

"So, I've, uh, been doing a lot of thinking." His voice sounded funny, like he'd rehearsed what he was about to say, or like he was expecting Jenny to be mad at him. She stopped walking and turned to face him. She zipped up her navy J.Crew hoodie.

"Me too."

Easy nodded. "Yeah?" He kept touching the pack of cigarettes in the back pocket of his jeans, like he was dying to have one, but the two of them were standing in the middle of campus, out in the open. "Well, good. Um, I just think that, it would be, you know, a good idea if . . . we broke up."

Even though she'd been preparing herself for the words, they still stung. But there was something else too, something she hadn't really expected to feel: relief. At least she had an answer now. She and Easy were over. She and Callie could be friends and roommates again. She nodded slowly, watching a dozen girls and boys in cable-knit sweaters rush down the front steps of one of the brick classroom buildings. "I think that would be for the best."

He looked at her tentatively, a little surprised, like he hadn't expected it to be this easy, and Jenny wondered if he had expected her to put up a fight, like Callie had when he'd broken up with her. The entire boys' dorm had heard her scream at him. But that wasn't Jenny's style, and besides, she wasn't angry. She was just sad. He shifted awkwardly from foot to foot. "We can, uh . . . still be friends, right?"

Jenny could tell it was hard for him to say something that clichéd and, well, lame. It sounded so awkward coming from his lips, and it almost made her laugh. "Sure," she told him.

Easy rubbed the bridge of his nose between his paint-splattered thumb and forefinger. "Really?" He peeked at her around his hand, and she felt his dark blue eyes exploring her face.

"Yeah, really." Jenny smiled up at him, even though her stomach was still in knots. Even though she already missed running her hands through his shaggy curls, or kissing his crooked lips, she just felt so relieved that she wasn't doing anything *wrong* anymore.

"Look . . . ," she trailed off, not having any idea what to say. She stared up at the brilliant blue sky and saw a fat brown owl zip between two trees. It made her think back to her first day at Waverly, when she'd practically been attacked by one. She kicked the toe of her red Dansko Mary Jane into the grass and wondered if things at Waverly *always* happened so fast. "I like you, Easy. That's not going to change, just because things are going to be . . . different."

"Yeah." He shook his head slowly, still looking surprised. Over his shoulder, Jenny spotted Tinsley striding along in a black minidress, her Fendi sunglasses perched coolly on the tip of her nose.

Easy bit his slightly chapped lips. "Seriously, you are probably the coolest girl I've ever met." He pushed up the cuffs of his gray, expensive-looking sweater, now covered with charcoal stains.

"I'll take that as a compliment." Jenny tilted her head toward Dumbarton. "Look, I'm going to go." She was feeling a little dizzy and wanted to talk to Brett. Maybe cry a little. And then go to practice, run around the field until her legs started to shake, and hit the field hockey ball really hard a few times. And then maybe tonight she and Brett and Callie and Kara could watch a movie in the lounge upstairs, something mindless and distracting, and eat burnt popcorn.

Easy paused and opened his mouth slightly, like he wanted to say something else, but no words came out. Jenny just gave him a little wave and stepped away. As her Mary Janes took her farther and farther away from the boy she'd thought she loved, she wasn't even tempted to turn back.

**Owl** Net   Instant Message Inbox

JennyHumphrey: It's official. Easy and I are over for good. He did the dirty work.

CallieVernon: Really? Wow. How are you feeling?

JennyHumphrey: I dunno. Sad. But relieved.

CallieVernon: Relieved?

JennyHumphrey: Yeah. I'm glad I can put our friendship first, finally.

CallieVernon: Want some cheering up? Margaritas tonight?

JennyHumphrey: That sounds poi-fect.

A WAVERLY OWL DOES NOT PASS NOTES IN CLASS— THAT'S WHAT TEXT MESSAGING IS FOR.

Brett stared at the blackboard in calculus late Wednesday morning, unable for the life of her to understand what all the graphs and figures meant. Dr. Goldstein, the absolutely ancient math teacher with a PhD from MIT, normally managed to slow down enough for her students to follow the complicated math processes she scratched across the board, but today Brett was completely lost. Maybe because she and some of the other girls had stayed up late last night in the downstairs common room, gossiping about boys and sex instead of studying. Something about the Women of Waverly meeting had really loosened everyone up, and as they sat around drinking Diet Cokes and eating Pirate's Booty, it had felt really, really good. Normally, all the Waverly girls seemed to be unconsciously—or consciously—competing with one another, always looking to see who had the newest bag or the sexiest shoes or the hottest boyfriend. But last night had been a release of so much tension, Brett felt like her life at Waverly had suddenly taken a turn for the better, regardless of the fact that this year, her love life had taken a dramatic turn—more like a nosedive—for the worse.

She simply could *not* get over the fact that Jeremiah had *slept* with someone else. If he had *kissed* his stupid crunchy chick, *that* would have been something she could understand. Kisses just happened. But sex? Sex was not something that *just happened*. There were a hell of a lot of steps to it—and a hell of a lot of chances for him to pause, and maybe, just maybe, you know, *not*.

Brett felt something poke her in the back through her thin, gray cowl-neck sweater. A beefy senior football player behind her held out a piece of notebook paper that had been folded a billion times into a tiny triangle. She raised her eyebrows at him, wondering why he was sending her a note when they'd never exchanged two words to each other. He twitched his head to his left, indicating, across the aisle, the figure of Heath Ferro, leaning back in his seat as if it were an armchair. He winked at Brett.

Great. She turned around and slowly unfolded the note beneath her desk, careful to keep the crinkling noise to a minimum. What was Heath doing passing notes? That was so junior high. In his surprisingly neat cursive, the note read, *I've seen a lot of kisses in my day, and there was DEFINITELY something to your kiss with Kara. Right?*

Brett felt her face flush. *What?* She resisted crumpling up the note into a tiny ball and chucking it back at Heath. Instead, she folded the note neatly back into its triangle and stuffed it into the pocket of her black wide-leg Sevens. She stared at the chalkboard and tried to concentrate on the figures.

Then she felt something vibrating silently next to her, and she slowly pulled her silver Nokia from the pocket of her maroon Waverly blazer hanging on her seat and casually hid it in her lap. It was a text message from Heath.

I M SERIOUS! IT LOOKED TOTALLY HOT. YOU MUST HAVE FELT SOMETHING.

She texted back to him, quickly. UR CRAZY.

Almost immediately her phone buzzed again. Brett glanced around the room and saw that most of the other students weren't paying attention to her but were either staring, mystified, at the board, or texting under their own desks. So much for cell phones not being allowed on campus—everyone used them during *class*. She read Heath's words. I DON'T BUY IT. YOU BOTH LOOKED . . . HOT. I THINK YOU SHOULD TRY IT AGAIN.

He was definitely crazy, Brett was sure. Or just swept away by the power of his fantasy life. He'd probably rushed home from the Women of Waverly meeting and bragged to all the guys that he'd gotten it on with an entire group of horny girls while the rest of them were busy playing Xbox or something. Without glancing back at Heath, she dropped her phone into her red-leather Kate Spade hobo bag, letting him know she was above further response.

After the bell rang, Heath managed to corner Brett right

outside the door. "Hey, I'm *serious*." He grabbed her by the arm and tugged her aside. "It really looked like you—"

"Look, I have no idea what you're talking about." Brett pushed him back against the wall and out of the stream of students elated to be done with classes for the morning. No one was paying attention to them, but Brett was still annoyed, though she tried not to look it. "People can hear you, you idiot."

Heath slung his arm across Brett's shoulder and opened his mouth to say something, but Brett cut him off, glancing around them and leaning in to speak closely to his ear. "I am *not* a . . . a lesbian."

"I'm not saying you are." Heath shrugged. "I don't pretend to understand the mystery that is female sexuality." The collar of his banana-colored Lacoste polo was half up and half down. "All I'm saying is that you should try kissing K"—Brett silenced him with a look—"*her* again and see how it feels."

Brett coolly flicked his arm off her shoulder.

Heath followed close behind her as Brett clacked down the marble hallway in her stacked Via Spiga heels. She could smell his aftershave as he leaned over her shoulder and whispered in her ear, "If you won't try that, you could always just go talk with Ms. Emory." He chuckled as he shuffled and squeaked his sneakers against the floor. Ms. Emory, the history teacher, was a known lady lover. "Maybe she has some words of wisdom."

Brett's irritation boiled up inside her, but she quickly remembered where she was once she felt a dozen eyes on her. There was no way she was going to continue a discussion of her sexuality—with Heath Ferro, of all people—in front of the entire school. Brett turned and poked her very red index finger into Heath's chest, almost flirtatiously. She caught his lazy green eyes with her own sharp ones and held his stare. She leaned in toward him, and his eyes moved to her lips, as if expecting them to kiss him.

"Don't. Mention. It. Again." Brett spoke slowly, enunciating each word, and Heath was left looking kind of mesmerized. *There,* she thought, triumphantly, wondering if she were somehow channeling Tinsley. She abruptly spun away from Heath and strode through the heavy front door and out into the bright autumn afternoon.

She tried to collect her thoughts but it felt like they were scattered all over the place—kind of like she'd been feeling all day. What she needed right now was to head to the library, pick up some Dorothy Parker—who was *not* a lesbian—and think about something other than herself for a while. A quote from her favorite author immediately came to mind, somewhat forebodingly: "It's not the tragedies that kill us, it's the messes."

She just hoped her life was not turning into one of the messes.

OwlNet   Instant Message Inbox

BennyCunningham:	I think Brett might be into Heath.
AlisonQuentin:	Um . . . and pigs fly.
BennyCunningham:	No, I'm serious! They were totally whispering to each other in the hallway today, and standing awfully close.
AlisonQuentin:	Maybe Heath just had something really interesting to say?
BennyCunningham:	Puhleeze. When was the last time that happened?
AlisonQuentin:	Ha. It must be love then!

OwlNet   Instant Message Inbox

EasyWalsh:	Where are you right now?
CallieVernon:	Now? I'm crossing the quad on my way to practice. Why?
EasyWalsh:	Stay right where you are, I'll be there in 2 minutes.
CallieVernon:	What? Why?
CallieVernon:	EZ!

14

A WAVERLY OWL IS NEVER LATE FOR PRACTICE
WITHOUT A GOOD FREAKING REASON.

After Easy's cryptic text, Callie dropped her phone into the pocket of her gray hooded Vassar sweatshirt and paused in the middle of the quad, wondering if she should even bother listening to him. It was chilly out, and the birds flying overhead in their wobbly V formation looked like they were already headed south. Smart birds. Callie was cold, but then she was always cold these days—it was the only drawback to getting skinnier. Not that she felt skinny in her thick fleecy sweatshirt and gray sweatpants.

Callie glanced around at all the bundled-up students, hurrying off to classes and dorms and sports classes, and felt suddenly aware that everyone around her was in motion while she was standing still. She immediately started doing her field hockey warm-up stretches, like it wasn't at all weird to be doing them in the middle of the quad instead of out on the field. Fuck. Why was Easy always doing this to her? And why was she always letting him? Damn him.

She fumed as she bent over in a V to stretch out her hamstrings, feeling the blood rush to her head. She walked her hands in toward her feet on the grass, and through her open legs saw Easy striding across the quad toward her. Even upside down, he looked completely gorgeous, and she could tell from the way his messenger bag thumped against his hip that he was rushing—to get to her. Callie quickly stood back up, her blood coursing through her veins. She shook out her mane of strawberry blond hair, which probably had grass or bugs or other nasties in it now from hanging upside down. Ew.

"What is it?" She asked brusquely as he approached, trying to sound irritated. She felt a little dizzy—which, she told herself, was from being upside down, not from the sudden appearance of Easy Walsh. He'd changed into a charcoal gray Michael Kors wool sweater, which was very adorably unlike him.

"I wanted to know if you'll be my model." His dark blue eyes examined her face in that way he had of seeming to take everything in at once, reading it all. His piercing gaze never missed a thing—he probably noticed the tiniest bits of grass in her hair, or how dry her skin was. And yet he was asking her to be his model? Even after the way she told him off this morning? "For art class," he clarified. "We have a project."

Callie smiled at the irony. Was this opposite day? For months—for practically a year, ever since they'd started dating—she had fantasized about her artsy boyfriend asking her to come out to the woods so that he could draw her. He could have built a sculpture of her out of clothes hangers and soup cans and she would have been thrilled. The Edie Sedgwick to his Warhol. The Beatrice to his Dante.

But he'd never asked her. Until now. Until now, when they couldn't possibly be a couple again. Not after all they'd been through, not after what she'd promised Jenny. She'd told Easy they were over and she'd meant it. Hadn't she?

"What would you need me to do?" she asked slowly, kicking the toe of her black Adidas cleats into the thick green grass of the quad.

Easy shook his head vehemently. "Nothing. Just pose for me." A smile broke out across his face. "Just be yourself."

Callie giggled. Be herself. Right. As long as she wasn't wearing sweatpants. "Are you sure you want . . . me?"

Easy didn't even pause to consider her question. "Yes." His gaze never left her face for a second.

She sighed. She couldn't stay angry at Easy forever. They were going to have to become friends at some point . . . and maybe that point was now. He needed someone to paint or draw for his class, and she could help him out, the way a friend would. And it wasn't like he was someone else's boyfriend, either—he and Jenny were through. So it would be completely platonic. "All right," she said with a tentative nod, keeping her voice even. So why were her palms sweating?

Easy sucked in his breath. "Awesome." He glanced up at her through his long dark eyelashes. "Do you have a lot of stuff to do tonight?"

"Stuff?" Callie repeated, amused.

"Yeah." He grinned. "You know, Latin. Calc. Stuff."

Callie was unable to keep a small smile from spreading across her face. Of course, homework, classes—the reasons they were even *here* at Waverly—fell under Easy's category of "stuff." "If you're asking if I have time tonight, then sure, whatever." Of course she had piles of homework, but suddenly the thought of sneaking away with Easy for a few hours felt like a breath of fresh air. "It's not like Ovid's going to mind if I break our date tonight."

"Wanna meet in the woods during dinner?" Easy pushed the sleeves of his sweater—probably the most expensive thing he owned—up to his elbows, stretching out the delicate cuffs.

"'Kay." She paused. "Snack bar afterward?" she added quietly. Dining services had a system where if you had to miss dinner— because of an away game, or a late practice, or whatever—you could use your dinner points at the Maxwell snack bar any time in the evening. Last year, she and Easy would always meet at the stables after practice and fool around for hours, until the dining hall was closed, and then, starving, head over to the snack bar and eat French fries and hummus wraps.

"I'll even buy you a strawberry milkshake," Easy promised, his eyes twinkling.

"Deal." She nodded her head definitively. Milkshakes were her favorite.

"So you'll meet me at my spot in the woods? It's—"

Callie cut him off. "I know where it is, Easy." Right by where the boys had gone hunting for mushrooms. She and Tinsley had walked out that way one day, and as soon as Callie had seen the little enclosed field with all the wildflowers and the funky rocks, she had *known* that that was Easy's secret spot. She'd thumbed through his sketchbooks sometimes, looking at his weird but beautiful drawings of trees and leaves and cigarette butts—he managed to make everything look beautiful.

And now he was going to draw her. Callie felt a little chill and heard the tweet of a whistle in the distance. "Shit," she muttered. "I've got to run. I'll see you later." She grabbed her lacrosse stick and dashed off toward the fields, knowing that Smail was going to make her do an extra lap around the field for being late.

But it was kind of worth it.

A WAVERLY OWL KNOWS THE BEST SURPRISES AREN'T ALL THAT SURPRISING.

Once the yellow taxi pulled away and left Brandon standing alone in front of St. Lucius's moss-covered front gate, he realized he'd gotten so carried away with his grand romantic gesture that he'd overlooked the most important part of the plan—he didn't know where to find Elizabeth. He took a few steps toward what looked like dorms, aware that the students milling about were definitely staring at him.

St. Lucius was like bizarro-Waverly—the same red brick, ivy, and brilliant oak trees surrounding the enormous quad, and yet not one familiar face. He'd bought a bunch of orchids in downtown Rhinecliff—roses were too conventional, daisies too boring—and now he suddenly felt a little self-conscious. Students were definitely gawking at him as he held the enormous cone of fuchsia and white flowers away from his chest so

as not to crush them. He felt like Forrest Gump with his box
of chocolates. Well, whatever. Had they never seen a guy bring
a girl flowers before?

Two girls in short jean skirts and matching purple regula-
tion St. Lucius blazers approached Brandon on the cobblestone
path. Judging from the worn-out look of their blazers, they had
to be upperclassmen. "Excuse me . . ." Brandon accosted them,
trying to look as inoffensive as possible. "Do you happen to
know which one is Elizabeth Jacobs's dorm?"

The girls, both thin, lanky blondes, exchanged glances. The
one with a navy velvet headband spoke first in a nasal, Long Island
accent. "Are those for her?" she asked, glancing at the flowers.

"Did her goldfish die or something?" the other asked, her
unseasonably tan forehead wrinkling in confusion.

Brandon was taken aback. Did they not have manners here?
"Uh, yeah, actually. They are." He raised his eyebrows pointedly, trying to remind the girls of his question. "But, um, no. I
think her, uh, goldfish is fine."

"That's really sweet." Velvet headband suppressed a giggle.
"She's in my dorm. Emerson." She pointed toward a white stone
building next to a thatch of birch trees with sunflower yellow
leaves. "Room 101—right inside, to the left."

"Thank you." Brandon headed that way, relieved that things
were working out. Over his shoulder he heard the second girl
trill out, "Good luck!"

Brandon made his way down the path, still sort of weirded
out by being in a place that looked like Waverly and smelled
like Waverly but wasn't. He paused briefly at the front door

of the building to read the quote, presumably from Emerson, inscribed above the doorway: DO NOT GO WHERE THE PATH MAY LEAD, GO INSTEAD WHERE THERE IS NO PATH AND LEAVE A TRAIL. "He couldn't help smiling as he opened the heavy green door. That quote reminded him of Elizabeth, and the way she seemed to do whatever the hell she wanted.

In front of room 101, he paused to collect himself, swiping one hand through his hair nervously. Then, just as he was about to knock, he heard the sounds of laughter coming from inside—*two* people's laughter. One sounded like Elizabeth, but the other was definitely a guy. What was going on? Panic shot through his veins, his get-the-hell-out-of-here instincts going into effect. He looked down stupidly at the orchids.

But then he thought, *What the hell?* He'd just spent forty dollars on flowers, and twenty dollars on a cab over here. What was he going to do, turn around and walk right out? Have the same cab driver come pick him up, along with his sad bouquet of flowers? Would Walsh do that? He didn't think so. *Have the balls to knock, Buchanan,* he told himself with a brisk nod. And so he raised his hand and knocked on the dark oak door, right under the Greenpeace bumper sticker.

The door opened quickly, and Elizabeth, looking like she was in the middle of a laugh, answered, wearing a pair of low-rise jeans that hung loosely at her hips and a slightly cropped gray T-shirt that revealed the tiny diamond stud in her belly button. Before Brandon had time to properly admire it, Elizabeth's face changed from surprise to delight, and she threw her arms around his neck, almost crushing the flowers.

"Brandon!" she cried just before giving him a huge, wet, hot French kiss. Well, that was more like it. When she finally pulled away, Brandon felt a little dizzy. Why had he waited so long to come and see her?

And then he noticed the guy sitting on her bed.

Elizabeth tugged Brandon into her room, which turned out to be a surprisingly spacious single. "Come on in!" she said gleefully, her loose blond hair just grazing her shoulders. "It's so good to see you." She seemed to remember the other guy. "Oh. This is Morgan. We were just studying." Elizabeth gave Morgan a raised eyebrow, and he quickly stood up. He was wearing a flannel T-shirt and a pair of corduroys with holes in the knees, and no shoes. Or socks. But he nodded politely at Brandon and didn't seem too upset about getting chased out.

"Later," he said, directed at both of them, before disappearing out the door. Where the hell were his shoes? Brandon wondered, staring at the royal blue shag rug. And where were the, uh, books? What exactly were they "studying"?

But before he could give the topic any more thought, Elizabeth was right at his side. "These are gorgeous," she cooed, closing her eyes and sniffing the orchids. "They look like poetry."

Brandon felt himself blushing. "Glad you like them. Roses seemed a little too conventional." He watched as she took the flowers out of their wrapping and delicately placed them in a half-full Nalgene water bottle sitting on her computer desk. Well, that was one way to do it.

"You know me already, don't you?" She gave him a knowing look before setting the bottle down on her surprisingly neat desk. She quickly returned to Brandon's arms and pressed her soft lips to his cheek. "Thank you," she murmured throatily.

Brandon closed his eyes for a moment, then opened them again. "Uh, I like your room." His eyes raced around the high-ceilinged space. Everything about it seemed sexy and Elizabeth-like, from the sleek iMac on her desk to the disorganized stack of Post-it-filled poetry books on her nightstand to the navy-and-turquoise tapestry thumbtacked to the wall. On the bulletin board were photos of Elizabeth all over the world, backpacking through Europe, on safari in Africa, even one on the Great Wall of China. And he couldn't help but notice lots of pictures of her partying with friends—who happened to be mostly male. She sure seemed to have a lot of guy friends.

Elizabeth placed her palms against Brandon's chest, and with a devious smile on her pretty face, pushed him down onto the soft cottony comforter on the bed. "It was totally sweet of you to come all the way over here." She lay down next to him and started stroking his chest. "I've been thinking about you all week," she purred. Her dirty blond hair was pulled back with tiny blue plastic barrettes, the kind that little girls usually wear, and her wide-set brown eyes sparkled with amusement.

"Oh, yeah?" Brandon couldn't help feeling that, well, maybe that other guy—what was his name? Morgan? What kind of girly name was that, anyway?—was no big deal. After all, Elizabeth had kissed Brandon right in front of him, so she clearly wasn't worried about his feelings. And now, as Elizabeth was nibbling on Brandon's ear, she clearly wasn't thinking about Morgan. So why should he? Right? *Riiiight.*

OwlNet

TinsleyCarmichael: Hey sexy. Whatcha doin'?

JulianMcCafferty: Headed to squash practice. You?

TinsleyCarmichael: I'm being deviant and skipping tennis. Heading back to my empty room in Dumbarton now. . . . Hint, hint.

JulianMcCafferty: Do you still have my lighter?

TinsleyCarmichael: Uh, what?

JulianMcCafferty: Never mind.

TinsleyCarmichael: Just come over, okay? I'll make you forget about your lighter. And hurry. I've been thinking about you all day. . . .

JulianMcCafferty: I'll be there in thirty seconds.

A WAVERLY OWL KNOWS THAT THE BEST WAY TO GET
OVER SOMEONE IS TO OBSESS OVER SOMEONE ELSE.

"So, um, Justin Timberlake or John Mayer?" Jenny asked
a little shyly as she and Callie trundled home from field
hockey practice in the early evening light, a cool breeze
tousling their sweat-dampened ponytails and sending brightly
colored leaves scuttling their way. Jenny's legs were pleasantly
exhausted from the exercise—Smail had run them hard today
in preparation for their game this weekend against St. Lucius,
whose field hockey team was Waverly's league rival. After about
ten minutes of warm-up drills, Jenny and most of the girls had
shed their Adidas track pants and sweatshirts, despite its feeling about twenty degrees out. It felt good now, as Jenny's heart
rate was returning to normal and the chilly breeze cooled her
still-hot skin. Brett had been a no-show at practice, and for
some reason it didn't feel at all awkward when Jenny and Callie
headed back to the dorm together alone. She felt like they'd

really been getting to know each other this past week, and not just because of the silly questions Jenny was asking her now. (Coke or Pepsi: "Diet Pepsi." Cats or dogs? "Cats, but only black ones." Kirsten Dunst or Scarlett Johannson: "Kirsten, but with Scarlett's voice.")

"So?" Jenny prompted. "Justin Timberlake or John Mayer?" she repeated.

Callie, still wearing her grass-stained sweatpants, her sweat-shirt tied loosely around her thin waist, twirled her Brine field hockey stick in one hand and snorted with laughter. "Are we talking music, or, like, who I'd rather make out with?"

Jenny tilted her orange Nalgene bottle and let the last drops of water trickle into her mouth. "Make out with. Definitely," she clarified.

"No contest." Callie swatted at a pebble with her stick, sending it ricocheting through the grass. "Justin Timberlake looks like he'd know exactly how to kiss me. Mmm."

Two months ago, Jenny would have been mortified by the idea of walking across a campus full of boys—cute, well-dressed, smart boys—and perfect, preppy, pretty girls, in a grass-stained T-shirt and gym shorts. But now she couldn't have cared less. It didn't matter. This was the boarding school way of life—wholesome, healthy, natural, and sometimes sweat-filled. She loved it.

"Really?" Jenny's stomach rumbled, reminding her that she was starving. "I'd definitely go for John Mayer. I guess I like . . ." She awkwardly trailed off, realizing she had just been about to say *that dark, sensitive, artsy type.* I.e., that Easy Walsh type. Not like she couldn't mention Easy, exactly—they'd talked about him plenty of times by now—but more like she didn't want to ruin the mood by bringing him in. Jenny bent down to tie her shoelace, pretending that was the reason she'd forgotten to complete her sentence.

Callie nodded absently as she climbed the front steps of the dorm. "Hey, I'm going to go in, okay? I've got to jump in the shower before heading to the, uh, library."

"Sure." Jenny responded equally absently, noticing someone moving behind one of the emerald green, carved topiaries that lined the wall of Dumbarton. It was *Julian*. Hanging out around the girls' dorm again. Jenny waved goodbye to Callie and headed toward the bushes. Despite all her thoughts about being sweaty as a wholesome, natural part of boarding school life, she quickly pulled the elastic from her hair and shook her head, letting her dark curls fall around her shoulders—that was a little better at least.

Julian was standing there with his hands in his pockets, leaning against the ivy-covered wall, looking a little flustered. He was wearing a pale green T-shirt that said, in retro yellow letters, IT'S NOT WHAT YOU'RE THINKING, and an unzipped royal blue track jacket with white stripes down the sleeves.

"Hark!" Jenny said, holding her field hockey stick out like a sword, the tip pointed directly at the lettering on Julian's chest. They'd just finished *Hamlet* in Miss Rose's class, and she was still in a Shakespearean state of mind. "Who goes there?"

He raised his eyebrows and did a Humphrey Bogart kind of voice. "We've got to stop meeting like this."

"Hey, I live here." Jenny grinned and retracted her hockey stick. She glanced around her but no one was approaching. First she'd been talking to Julian in a broom closet, now behind a bush. It was kind of fun—where would he pop up next? And *why* was he here again? "What's your excuse? Are you looking for your—what was it? Your *lighter*—again?"

"Funny girl." He shrugged his shoulders, and a ray of setting sunlight burst through the elegantly sculpted bush he was standing behind, lighting up his features from behind. "But, no. I was just, you know, passing by."

The dramatic lighting made the shapes of his face stand out even more than they normally did, and Jenny noticed for the first time how strong the planes of his cheekbones were, how deep-set his dark eyes were, how crooked his nose was. It was the kind of face that would look great in marble, she thought. It took her a moment to realize it was her turn to speak again—so much for her brilliant Shakespearean repartee. "So, uh, what am I thinking?" she asked, hoping her face was a cute rosy-cheeked red, and not an are-you-having-a-heart-attack red.

Julian smiled at her but looked kind of confused, like he'd lost the trail of conversation. "Uh, what?" He leaned forward.

"Your shirt." Jenny pointed toward it and raised her eyebrows. "You've probably been getting that all day."

Julian glanced down at his chest as understanding washed over his face. "Actually, I had my Sea World T-shirt on today." He tilted his head and shrugged his shoulders, which made him look kind of like a little kid. "I just changed." The dimple near his lips deepened.

A giggle burst from Jenny's lips. Something about Julian was just so friendly and open—it was nice to flirt with him. It took her mind off other tall, handsome boys. "I know this is going to sound totally crazy, but would you be at all interested in being a model for my art class project?" She really hoped he wouldn't think she was flirting with him—because she wasn't. Not really. "I think you'd make a great subject."

He looked completely taken aback and glanced around him. Yikes! She hoped he wasn't going to take it the wrong way. "Uh, right now? Behind the bushes?"

"No!" Jenny pushed an unruly lock of hair behind her ear. She couldn't believe she was standing here talking to a totally cute guy when she was in desperate need of a shower. At least he probably couldn't smell her from where he was hiding. "I didn't mean right now. Maybe tomorrow?"

"I don't know if I've ever been a piece of art before." His fingers played with a branch of the bush he was stuck next to. "Sounds kinda cool."

"Sweet." Jenny tapped her hockey stick against the brick wall. "I'll e-mail you about a time." She smiled coyly. "That is, if I don't see you in the broom closet before then."

She walked inside to the sound of his laughter. As she climbed the stairs to room 303, she realized that there would definitely be other cute boys on campus to distract her from Easy. Maybe Callie could find someone to distract her from the unforgettable Easy Walsh, too. Everything was finally working out just the way it was supposed to.

OwlNet   Instant Message Inbox

TinsleyCarmichael: It's been more than thirty seconds.

TinsleyCarmichael: Are you still coming over?

TinsleyCarmichael: Julian?

18

A WAVERLY OWL KNOWS HOW TO APPRECIATE
MOTHER NATURE—ESPECIALLY WITH ANOTHER OWL.

*W*hat am I doing? What am I doing? Callie paused at the edge of the path to the boathouse, right at the spot where Easy had instructed her to turn off, the sky just beginning to glow orange. Her stomach rumbled a little, reminding her that she was skipping dinner. But she was too nervous and keyed up to eat anything anyway. After practice, she'd raced to shower off the sweat and grime their long practice had left her covered in, then dressed carefully. She had no idea what constituted appropriate clothing for a modeling session in the woods with her ex-boyfriend, and after deliberating for about twenty minutes she'd had to force herself to just get dressed already. Easy had asked to paint her, after all, and so he must want her to show up looking like herself. If that meant wearing expensive, slightly inappropriate clothing, so be it.

And so here she was, in her tight-fitting black Theory trou-
sers, high-heeled pointy-toed boots, and black Vince scoop-neck
sweater with a neckline just high enough not to be inappropriate. Her still-damp hair was curling slightly at the ends
and making her feel even colder. She zipped her red quilted
down vest up to her chin, the rabbit-fur lining making her nose
twitch, and stepped off the path, the heels of her boots sinking
slightly into the mossy undergrowth. She reminded herself of
her resolution with Jenny and how she'd just lied to her, saying
she was in a rush to get to the library. She was not going to let
this thing with Easy go beyond a friendship. In fact, for that
reason, she'd purposely not shaved her legs in the shower—leg
stubble always made her feel so unsexy, and she felt like she
might need to harness that unsexy feeling when spending time
alone with Easy in the woods.

She made her way through the woods, stepping carefully
over branches and enjoying the way the dry leaves crumpled
beneath her feet. Callie inhaled the fresh, leafy air and wished
she were a more outdoorsy person—it might be kind of fun,
as long as it didn't mean she had to wear ugly hiking boots or
wear that awful all-natural deodorant crap. She came up to the
small clearing that she'd guessed was Easy's secret spot, and
sure enough, there he was, crouched down in front of a bunch
of tubes of paint scattered on the grass. She just stood there for
a moment, staring at him, taking in the scene. He looked so
natural out here, and even from how far away she was, she could
read in his movements a relaxed happiness that she only really
got to see when he was around Credo.

Then he looked up and saw her, and his face dissolved into a huge crooked grin. "Hey," he said, standing up and brushing off his hands on his already dusty dark jeans. "What do you think?" He held his arms out to indicate the clearing.

Callie approached slowly, aware that even the sight of Easy doing something so simple as holding his arms out was making all of her old feelings for him come back. Fuck. This was definitely going to be harder than she thought, unshaved legs or no. "It's nice," she commented politely. "Where are the flowers?"

"Well, it *is* October."

"What, there are no flowers in fall?" she asked petulantly, already feeling herself slide into the slightly contrary attitude that Easy had always gotten off on. She didn't mean to—it just felt so . . . *natural*. "That's stupid."

Easy laughed. His dark blue eyes crinkled up at the edges, and Callie could tell from his expression that he wanted to kiss her, the way he had done a thousand times—which broke her heart. Yes, she'd been hoping with every ounce of her being that he would realize how stupid he had been and come running back to her, throwing himself at her feet and begging for forgiveness. She missed him. She missed his deep laugh that came from somewhere down in his belly, the way he raised one eyebrow slightly when he thought she was bullshitting him about something. "Whatever. The leaves will make a pretty cool background, especially once the sun starts to set," he said.

Callie felt Easy's gaze wash over her. Did he look at *all* of his models this way? A few weeks ago, Tinsley had insinuated that Easy had been out in this very painting spot with Jenny. That hurt. No way was she going to let him hurt her again, not like that. Callie shook her head disdainfully. "So, what do you want me to do here? Stand in front of the leaves?"

Easy scratched his neck and narrowed his eyes, focusing intently on her face. Callie felt her stomach flop but tried not to let her face betray her feelings. "I want to do some sketches first to sort of get some ideas out." He picked up an enormous sketch pad and pulled a stubby pencil from behind his ear. "So maybe just sort of sit on the rock for now?"

Callie eyed the rock. She'd sort of thought modeling would mean stretching out on a luxurious, velvet chaise lounge, maybe just wearing some silky robe casually thrown about her. Something *Titanic*-like, the heart of the ocean around her neck. Not perching on a dirty, uncomfortable rock in the middle of October when it was freezing out and she had to wear her puffy red vest with the fur-trimmed hood. If Easy wanted to paint an Eskimo, he could've looked one up in the library. Well, whatever. *He* was the artist. She eased herself down on top of the rock, hooking her stacked heels on a small ledge. "How's this?"

"You look like you're pissed to be sitting on a rock," Easy said with a knowing smile. "Or being forced this close to nature."

She knew Easy kind of got off on the fact that she was a bit of a sheltered princess. "Fine." Callie pivoted on the rock and leaned over, throwing her arms around it in a giant bear hug. "Oh, rock, I love you so much and I am so excited to be sitting on you, even though you are cold and dirty and uncomfortable." She tried to put the most lovesick look on her face that she could manage and blew kisses at it. Out of the corner of her eye, she could see Easy bent over with laughter.

Callie got really into it, striking a series of exaggerated poses around the rock, then getting up and pouncing on the birch trees. "O trees, o nature," she said throatily, wrapping her arms around a skinny white birch tree and fake-kissing it, bringing her lips as close to the peeling white bark as she could bear without thinking too much about the bugs that lived in it. She tossed her hair like a real spotlight-loving prima donna and watched as Easy's pencil flew across the page.

But when she tried to pull away from the tree, she felt a sharp tug on her scalp. "Ow!" she cried, reaching up toward her head. Her hair was stuck on a branch. Fucking nature.

"Are you okay?" Easy was at her side in seconds, his sketch pad and pencil abandoned on the ground. "Don't pull." As he reached over her to try and untangle her hair from the branch, she caught the familiar smell of his Ivory soap mingled with musty, stable-y smells. She glanced up at him, tenderly working on her hair, trying not to pull against her scalp, and she felt her hazel eyes fill up with fat tears.

"There." Easy pushed the branch away from her head. "You're free." And then he saw her face. "Did I hurt you?"

Don't cry, don't cry, don't cry, she chastised herself, but that just made the tears spill over. She covered her face with her hands. "Yes," she said softly, meaning it. Not her hair though, her heart. She tried to turn away from him, but he was too quick. His strong arms pulled her to his chest before she could protest, and once her body was against his, she just melted into the scratchy wool of his sweater. *Easy*.

She felt his cheek resting again her head. "I know. I'm so sorry, but I swear I will never, ever hurt you again," he whispered as he kissed the spot where her hair had gotten snagged by the tree. She had to close her eyes. "I love you, Callie. I really do."

And before she could stop to think about it any more, she kissed him. His cheek first, then his eyebrows, his nose, and finally, his soft, warm, waiting mouth.

19

A WAVERLY OWL KEEPS HER LIPS SEALED. OR NOT.

Brett glanced down at her calculus homework, unable to concentrate on the lines of letters and numbers. She'd come over to Kara's for some study time, but so far hadn't been able to focus. She bit the end of her pen.

"What did you get for number twelve? It's $n^2 + 2n$, right?" Kara asked from her perch in her red butterfly chair, her calculus textbook balanced on her thighs. She pressed the eraser end of her pencil to her forehead, right between her eyes. "Because if it's not, I'm going to take this book over to Dr. Goldstein's house right now and set it on fire on her front lawn, right next to her freaky little gnomes." Dr. Goldstein lived in one of the small white clapboard faculty houses at the edge of campus, and her lawn was peppered with brightly colored ceramic gnomes that would probably have been stolen by frustrated calculus students if not for Spike, Dr. Goldstein's Rottweiler, which patrolled her yard, drooling and growling.

"Good thing you're right, because they say Spike can smell pissed-off student blood a hundred yards away." Brett giggled. "A man-eating dog and garden gnomes—what is Dr. Goldstein's *deal,* anyway?"

Kara leaned forward conspiratorially, slamming her heavy textbook closed. "Didn't you hear that, like, two years ago, she started hooking up with some genius graduate student from Caltech who was interviewing her for his senior thesis?" Kara's eyes widened and she drummed her bitten-down fingernails against her notebook. "Apparently, he lives in the city now and comes up every weekend to, you know, *interview* her."

Brett gasped. Dr. Goldstein's shirts were always buttoned wrong and she wore mismatched socks. Brett had taken it as a sign of her absentminded brilliance—but maybe it was because she was up late the night before, getting some from her hunky young grad student? "Isn't she, like, a thousand? I definitely would not have guessed that she was—you know—having wild, passionate sex every weekend."

Kara let her pencil fly across the room so that it landed right in Brett's lap. "I say more power to her."

"Whatever. I've been with younger guys and older guys, and I think they're all the same breed of idiot." Brett picked up Kara's yellow number 2 pencil and examined it. No teeth marks. Brett's pencils were all chewed up at the ends, no matter how gross she knew the habit was. Someone had told her once—probably Heath—that chewing on pencils was a sign that you were sexually repressed.

"That sounds so pessimistic," Kara said wistfully, dropping

her calc book onto the floor and standing up to stretch, her gray American Apparel T-shirt rising to reveal a thin sliver of pale stomach above her black drawstring lounge pants. "I'm sure there are some good guys out there. Like, one or two."

"Right." Brett ran her hand across Kara's bright-blue-and-red Batgirl bedspread, smoothing out the wrinkles she'd made by sprawling out across it for the past hour. God, how much easier would life be if she had a single? No more nutjob Tinsley to have to tiptoe around, worrying about when her next eruption was due. And Kara's room was just so . . . *nice*. It was so neat and clean, and smelled like new books and incense. She even had a leafy green plant dangling from her curtain rod. "They just happen to live in, like, outer Mongolia or something."

Kara spun the dial on her stereo, turning up the volume on the new Aimee Mann CD. She did a few dance steps on the hardwood floor, looking kind of silly but totally unself-conscious. Brett envied her that. "And they probably don't have Internet there, do they?"

Brett smiled as she watched Kara prance around her room. Until last weekend, Kara had hung out by herself—but after the lockdown party, she had sort of unquestioningly been taken in by the Waverly elite. Brett had noticed both Alison Quentin and Sage Francis wearing clothes from Kara's closet this week, and Heath and some other guys had been seen hanging out with her at various times. And yet she still sat with Yvonne Stidder and some of the other loners at dinner. To Brett, that was just so unimaginably cool. "Are you saying you wouldn't date someone who lived in outer Mongolia and didn't have Internet access?" Brett teased. "That's discrimination."

Kara nodded with a wicked grin. "Sure am—no cybersex, no deal!"

Brett laughed loudly. It felt good to laugh, to forget about Jeremiah and how he had lied to her, and Mr. Dalton and how he had lied to her too. Forgetting guys was totally blissful.

"Ladies?" There was a stern knock on Kara's open door and Angelica Pardee, with her faded flowered bathrobe bunched tightly around her waist, glared into the room disapprovingly. "It's late. Time to turn in."

"Sorry, Mrs. Pardee," Kara answered sweetly, quickly turning her music back down. "We just have a few more calc problems to finish off, and then we're done."

Pardee cinched her belt tighter around her waist and sniffed the air disapprovingly, but not seeing any banned candles in sight, she seemed satisfied. "Not much longer."

Brett got up and closed the door behind her. The hallway had already quieted down after Pardee's patrol, and Brett was suddenly very aware of the fact that she and Kara were completely alone. "So, what about that last problem?" She returned to Kara's bed and perched gingerly on the edge, her pulse racing. It was totally Heath's fault for putting the thought into her head this afternoon, but she couldn't help it now—she just kept thinking about the tiny kiss that she and Kara had shared.

Kara scooped up her calc notebook and sat down on the bed. The stereo was still playing, but quietly, and there were no noises from the hallway. It kind of felt like she and Kara were the only people—or at least the only sane people—awake right now. Kara leaned over and placed her finger on Brett's notebook. "I think you've got it." She flipped a page of the math book, then glanced up at Brett. "It's the summation, right?"

Brett nodded, feeling kind of dazed.

"Are you okay?" Kara asked, swiping at a strand of light brown hair that had fallen in her face. "Are you still thinking about Dr. Goldstein and her boy toy?"

"No!" Brett laughed and grabbed for her bottle of Evian on Kara's bedside table. "Don't give me nightmares."

"Then what are you thinking about?" Kara asked, gently, her greenish-brown eyes curious.

Could she honestly tell her? What if Kara thought she was a freak and demanded Brett get the hell out of her room? But she knew Kara wouldn't do that. Everything with her seemed so natural—even this didn't seem like a big deal. "Umm . . . about the meeting last night."

Kara finally blushed, but only a little, like she knew immediately what Brett was referring to. "Oh." She played with the edge of her notebook paper, waving it back and forth. "That was . . ." She shrugged her slim shoulders, and a small grin crept onto her face. "Kinda fun."

Brett pressed her lips together. "Yeah."

A moment passed, as they looked at each other. Brett noticed a tiny freckle just below Kara's pale pink lips. And then Brett leaned in, over the sprawled-open pages of mathematical problems and pencil scrawls, and pressed her mouth slowly to Kara's.

Their lips touched softly, and Brett closed her eyes, letting her mouth move almost imperceptibly against Kara's. It wasn't the sort of sloppy devouring she was used to from Jeremiah. Kara's mouth was neat and small, and in a totally weird way, it was sort of like . . . kissing herself.

It was nice.

A WAVERLY OWL CAN CONFIDE IN HER ROOMMATE . . .
RIGHT?

Jenny pounded up the stairs of Dumbarton on Wednesday night after spending the after-dinner hours in the library, working on her first long paper for European history. After three grueling hours, she was happy to come back to her room again. Finally, she didn't have to tiptoe around Callie anymore. They were both beyond that, and it felt exhilarating. She tried not to think too much about missing Easy—she just kind of hoped that she could push that sadness aside until one day it wasn't really sadness anymore, just nostalgia. It wasn't the end of the world, she kept telling herself. And it wasn't like she wasn't ever going to see him again. Maybe she could still go horseback riding with him? And she'd still get to be in art class with him and joke around and see his FOOD NOT BOMBS T-shirt. She just wouldn't get to . . . kiss him.

Anyway. She paused in front of the door of 303, reading a

note scrawled in red marker across her dry-erase board: *Tomorrow night = 1. Coffee 2. Study 3. Gossip 4. All of the above? xo, Brett*. Brett hadn't shown up for practice today, but because she was junior class prefect, all she had to do was hint at some sort of important meeting and Smail let her skip, no questions asked.

Jenny opened the door quietly, half expecting Callie to be in bed already. But she brightened when she saw her roommate was still awake. In fact, she was standing in front of a completely empty closet in a pink tank top and white girly boxers folded over at the waist, staring into it, all of her expensive clothes stacked in teetering piles on top of the spare bed, threatening to spill over at any moment.

"You're cleaning?" Jenny blurted out, surprised. The room looked like an exclusive SoHo boutique had just exploded.

"Huh?" Callie glanced over her thin shoulder at Jenny and blinked a few times. "Oh. Yeah, I guess . . . I just got this urge." Callie's eyes ran over the towering stacks of clothing like she couldn't remember how they'd gotten there. "I guess I didn't think it was such a big project."

"Why don't you just leave it?" Jenny suggested awkwardly. "Finish it tomorrow?" She dropped her heavy bag onto the floor and sank down on her own bed, grateful that she'd soon be curled up under her father's old quilt that still sort of smelled like their apartment on 99th Street and West End Avenue.

Callie bit her lip and fingered the sleeve of a transparent, muslin-y blouse on the top of one precarious stack. "But the room is a total disaster," she finally answered, a little poutily.

"I don't mind if you don't." Jenny propped herself up on her elbows and kicked off her pink Chuck Taylors. They thudded gently against the hardwood floor. "It's not like it's usually clean," she added with a giggle. The room, even with only the two of them in all that space, always seemed to be littered with empty Diet Pepsi bottles (Callie's) and half eaten mini-bags of Baked Doritos (Jenny's), and the spare desk was always buried under massive stacks of clean laundry, notebooks, old term papers, and various objects that were not needed at any precise moment. There was even a neatly folded tapestry that neither Jenny nor Callie laid claim to that had somehow appeared one day.

Callie bunched her hair into two fistfuls and tugged at it. Her arms looked as flimsy as plastic straws, and Jenny thought about how much she'd like to force-feed her roommate a cheeseburger. Maybe Callie was so out of it because she was starving? She didn't really know what she should do about that. Should she talk to Pardee? Suddenly she remembered the two Tootsie Pops she'd picked up at the snack bar. Jenny patted the pocket of her Waverly blazer and held out the two of them, like a peace offering.

Callie laughed, and Jenny mentally willed her to take one. She did, coming over to Jenny and taking the raspberry one shyly. "Thanks."

Jenny smiled. Maybe Callie just needed to take her mind off things. "Hey, you know that really tall, cute freshman?" she asked as she unwrapped her orange lollipop and stuck it on her tongue.

"Julian?" Callie answered with her mouth full of lollipop,

so that it came out sounding like "Mwwaniaw?" She pulled the
sucker from her mouth, her lips already tinged purple. "What
about him?"

"I don't really know." Jenny tucked her feet up next to her
on the bed and stuffed her folded pillow beneath her head.
"He just kind of . . . keeps showing up around the dorm. Like,
he was in the bushes outside when we got back from practice
today." She giggled, thinking about their funny conversation
when she'd found him. "And he was in the broom closet yesterday. Downstairs."

"Wait, he snuck into the dorm?" Callie's hazel eyes focused
on Jenny's face and lit up with excitement. She pulled the
lollipop out of her mouth and waved it at Jenny. "Do you think
he, like, *likes* you?"

"Oh, definitely not," Jenny said quickly, her cheeks turning
pink. She hated it when people suggested someone liked her
and she didn't really think it was true. "I really have no idea
what he was doing. He made up some lame excuse about looking for something."

"Right." Callie rushed over to Jenny's bed, feeling very
sisterly all of a sudden, and sat down near Jenny's yellow-socked
feet. "I bet he was looking for *you*!" She felt energized just thinking about it. How perfect would that be? What Jenny needed
was some cute guy to come out of nowhere and sweep her off
her feet and make her forget that she had ever even known a boy
named Easy Walsh. And Julian was totally hot—maybe a little
tall for Jenny, but clearly she liked them tall. Callie patted her
roommate's feet excitedly.

"No, that's totally silly. It wasn't like that." Jenny's whole mouth was orange from her lollipop and Callie had to giggle. She looked like she was just a little kid, albeit a really adorable one. And Julian was, what? A freshman? He couldn't be more perfect for her. "But I mean, we had this really nice kind of flirty chemistry thing going on." She sat up in bed, her eyes slightly dreamy, and toyed with a long brown curl.

"Maybe you'll run into him tomorrow?" Callie tried not to sound too eager—she didn't want Jenny to suspect that she had ulterior motives or anything. A tiny wave of guilt passed over her as she realized that she was already lying to Jenny by not telling her about Easy. But it was for her own good, right? It would devastate Jenny if she knew that Easy and Callie were, kind of . . . Easy and Callie again.

Jenny stood up and opened a dresser drawer, pulling out a pair of cozy-looking navy Nick and Nora pj bottoms, the white stick of the Tootsie Pop extending out of her mouth like some kind of über-skinny cigarette. She glanced at Callie and smiled devilishly. "Well, I did ask if he wanted to model for my art class project. So . . . I probably will see him tomorrow."

"That's awesome!" Callie exclaimed. She couldn't help it— she exploded off the bed and gave Jenny a huge hug. *Please, please, please, please, please let Jenny and Julian fall madly in love!* "Something's totally going to happen between you two. I can feel it!"

She just hoped it would happen *fast*.

 **Owl**Net

From: JennyHumphrey@waverly.edu
To: RufusHumphrey@poetsonline.com
Date: Wednesday, October 9, 9:29 P.M.
Subject: Happy Wednesday!

Hi Dad,

Didn't mean to sound like I was in a funk the other day—I think I was just a little drained after an excruciating Latin class. (But you should hear me recite Cicero now—I've come far in a month!)

Things are totally going well. As always, I'm loving my art classes. I can't believe I get credit for drawing. We just got a new assignment today that I'm hoping to tackle tomorrow—with the help of a cute boy who's going to model for me. (I love school!)

We're reading Virginia Woolf's *To the Lighthouse* in English class. Dad, I can't believe you let me make it through fifteen years of life on this planet without ever reading this. How could you?? =)

Miss you. Have an extra cupcake at Bernard's for me (if you haven't already)!

Your favorite daughter and xoxo,

Jenny

 **OwlNet**

 Owl Net

From: JennyHumphrey@waverly.edu
To: Julian McCafferty@waverly.edu
Date: Wednesday, October 9, 9:45 P.M.
Subject: Be a model citizen . . .

. . . or at least a model Owl. If you're still up for being part of my art project, will you meet me tomorrow in the art studio? Six-thirtyish maybe, or 6:45?

Let me know. Looking forward to seeing what T-shirt you'll wear next.

—Jenny ;)

21

A WAVERLY OWL IS ALWAYS A GRACIOUS WINNER—
ESPECIALLY WHEN SHE'S CHEATED.

Thursday morning, Tinsley was buzzed into Marymount's Stansfield Hall office. It was an enormous room on the second floor with huge bay windows that had sweeping views of the entire campus and, in early October, the flaming colors of the autumn foliage. As she strode across the dark mahogany floor and onto the distinguished, threadbare Turkish carpet in her Stuart Weitzman lace-up brown leather boots, Marymount stood up from his shockingly neat desk. It wasn't that it was empty—it was in complete geometric order. A large paper calendar was spread out in the middle, filled with carefully penned-in appointments and notes. Tiny cups of pens, dishes of paper clips, a tape dispenser, and a stapler were all lined up as if in military formation, ready at any moment to attack. Even the silver picture frame of the dean's family was angled perfectly toward his chair to allow his guests to just catch a glimpse of his blond, angelic-looking wife and children. *Interesante.* His wife was way prettier than Angelica freaking Pardee. Tinsley shook his outstretched hand.

"Ms. Carmichael," he said pleasantly, if a little efficiently. "What can I do for you today?"

Tinsley noticed he was wearing a floral-print tie, with a field of red and pink tulips. His prematurely balding secretary, Mr. Topkins, had been wearing one with yellow daisies. Weird. Tinsley sank into one of the antique chairs and crossed her legs, primly stretching the hem of her army green button-front shirtdress down over her knee. "I've been talking with Mrs. Feingold at the Rhinecliff Public Library about borrowing their copy of *It Happened One Night* to show at an upcoming Cinephiles event." That much was certainly true—she'd spent an hour listening to the elderly woman chew her ear off about how "debonair" Clark Gable was and how all the ladies in her day "swooned" over him.

"Ah!" Marymount exclaimed, leaning back in his chair and tapping his fingers against his temples. "Excellent film. That Claudette Colbert—what a charmer."

Tinsley nodded enthusiastically. "Exactly. So, as I was talking to Mrs. Feingold, she mentioned the fact that the library occasionally holds outdoor screenings, and they have all the equipment for it and would be willing to lend it to the Cinephiles." Marymount's face was becoming decidedly darker as she was talking, almost comically so, as if he had suddenly sucked on a lemon.

Tinsley plowed on regardless. "And so . . . I was hoping to

get permission for a special off-campus Cinephiles event. Mrs. Feingold also offered up the use of her old barn in town, as she says it would be perfect for screening the film on its side wall." That part was the fairly egregious lie—poor Mrs. Feingold probably would have swooned herself if she'd known how she was being implicated in this farce, yet Tinsley couldn't very well tell Marymount that the barn belonged to the liquor store guy.

Dean Marymount shook his head slowly and resolutely. "I'm afraid it is completely out of the question to grant permission for something like this." He ran his hand through his wispy, colorless hair and coughed. "The legal ramifications alone . . ." He was shaking his head faster now, like it was just such a phenomenally stupid idea he couldn't even believe Tinsley had bothered him with it. "But especially in light of all the trouble that has gone on here in the last few weeks." He looked sternly at her over the rims of his glasses. "It's simply not possible."

"I understand your reservations, sir," Tinsley answered politely, sitting forward in her chair and lowering her eyes humbly. Her knees trembled a little at what she was about to say, but she kept her voice steady. She'd been excited about this meeting all of yesterday, for this precise moment. After she said it, there would be no turning back. Marymount would hate her forever, if he didn't already. But was it fair that she and Callie should be punished for getting caught that weekend in Boston, drunk and half naked, and yet he, who was arguably the worst offender, cheating on his wife with Pardee, should go completely unscathed? Tinsley had been forced to move into a room with pain-in-the-ass Brett, and yet she had kept Marymount's secret. She was certainly entitled to some, ahem, fringe benefits of being his secret sharer.

And with that attitude, she plunged forward. "I know the school's policy against off-campus activities, but I can assure you that this would be *nothing* like the trip to Boston." She paused, staring at the toes of her boots as if she were completely contrite and not, in fact, blackmailing him. "Something like that would *never* happen again. . . . I guess *everyone* just got a little crazy that weekend and wasn't thinking about the ramifications of their actions."

There. She'd said it. Tinsley had thought and thought about the best way to say it, and had finally decided on veiling it enough so that Marymount would not be too humiliated or offended that he immediately expelled her. If she was subtle enough, she could give him an out—in his heart of hearts, he knew what she was saying, and she was allowing him to just play along with it and not so much think about it as actually being blackmailed. By one of his students. The silence lingered in the air, the ticking of the grandfather clock in the corner, and the pounding of her heart were the only sounds her ears picked up. Maybe he was just going to explode—and expel her? She would actually be kind of impressed if he did.

After a sufficiently awkward silence, Marymount cleared his throat, and Tinsley looked up eagerly, her face the picture of innocence. *Think Bambi,* she told herself. *Snow White. I have done nothing wrong. Let him see it.* She felt his eyes searching her face for something, but they didn't seem to find it. Finally, he sighed heavily. "And when were you hoping to have this event?"

Tinsley's heart leapt with joy. "This Friday—tomorrow, that is—would be perfect. I know it's short notice, but the weather is supposed to be terrific, and it just seems like a wonderful chance for this to happen before autumn really starts, you know?"

Marymount took another deep breath and squeezed the bridge of his nose between his thumb and index finger. Tinsley pretended not to notice what was going on with him and kept a pleasantly surprised and grateful expression on her face, squelching her triumphant elation. Always be a gracious winner. "I just want you to know, Ms. Carmichael"—Marymount's glance at the framed picture on his desk did not escape Tinsley's watchful eye—"that I am going to have to hold you *fully responsible* for anything that goes wrong."

She nodded gravely, already thinking about making out with Julian in the barn. "Nothing will go wrong, sir, but I am willing to be responsible for anything that may."

"And also," he continued, his voice unwavering, his eyes meeting Tinsley's directly for the first time in several minutes, "this is going to be the *last* time something like this occurs. Understood?"

"Perfectly." She nodded, even though everyone knows that the first time, for anything, is rarely the last.

OwlNet

To: Undisclosed recipients
From: TinsleyCarmichael@waverly.edu
Date: Thursday, October 10, 12:38 P.M.
Subject: *It Happened One Night*—i.e., tomorrow

Dear lucky invitees,

You are cordially welcomed to join Cinephiles for a special off-campus party and screening of *It Happened One Night* at the Miller farm in Rhinecliff, tomorrow (Friday) night at 7 P.M.

Dean Marymount has graciously allowed us to hold this special showing of the film in honor of his undying love of the great Claudette Colbert. Be sure to send him a thank-you e-mail on Saturday morning. That is, if you're not still hammered.

Transportation: I trust you are all inventive enough to work that out on your own.

Au revoir, mes enfants,

Tinsley

From: JulianMcCafferty@waverly.edu
To: JennyHumphrey@waverly.edu
Date: Thursday, October 10, 12:40 P.M.
Subject: Re: Be a model citizen . . .

J,

I'm still down to help out with your project. I'll be there at 6:30.

So you like the T-shirts, huh? I'll try to surprise you. In the words of
Right Said Fred, I'm too sexy for my shirt. . . .

Just kidding—I promise I'll come fully clothed. See you later.

—(the other) J

A WAVERLY OWL DOES NOT OVERTHINK MATTERS OF THE HEART. EXCEPT WHEN SHE DOES.

Despite the soothing whir of the cappuccino machine and the Dar Williams music playing at CoffeeRoasters, the tiny coffee shop in downtown Rhinecliff, on Thursday afternoon, Brett's whole body was atwitter. Across from her, Jenny was bent over her textbook, happily highlighting away. The people who hung out at CoffeeRoasters were of the soy-milk-ordering, organic-pumpkin-muffin-eating variety, and although Brett was not crunchy by any stretch of the imagination, she kind of liked being around people who were.

But even with the study-inducing vibe—not to mention caffeine—all she could think about was what had happened last night with Kara. *The kiss.* Brett had never kissed a girl before, not seriously, but she'd never been a prude, either, so she just hadn't thought about it one way or another. She could think of plenty of times when at parties, drunken girls tended to get all huggy and kissy, but she'd always thought that was mainly for the benefit of the horny boys watching. Kissing Kara was different. First of all, no one was watching, and second of all, they did it because they wanted to, and not because they were drunk.

If Brett had been worried that things would be awkward between her and Kara after their little make-out session, she needn't have wasted her energy. When Brett had run into Kara coming out of the bathroom this morning, a lock of wet hair clinging to her cheek, the two of them had instantly grinned at each other—the shy, knowing grin that exists only between two people who share a very exciting secret. And nothing was really different at lunch either. They chatted as they would have before, except everything was a little more charged, each of them knowing what the other was thinking about, and no one else in the world having a clue. It was definitely exciting. Maybe they stood a little closer to each other, but not enough that anyone else would notice.

Brett kept glancing up at Jenny, sitting across the tiny, slightly sticky table from her, her yellow highlighter poised over her biology textbook, ready to attack. She had to keep biting her cheek to prevent herself from spilling her guts to Jenny right now. But . . . Jenny *had* kept her secret about Dalton, after all. She could certainly be trusted. And Brett really felt like if she didn't tell someone about this, she might spontaneously combust.

Jenny looked up questioningly from her book before Brett could think of another reason not to spill. Her chocolate brown eyes were just so warm and friendly, and the freckles sprinkled across her slightly upturned nose just so reassuring and nonjudgmental, Brett couldn't fight it any more. She flipped her book down on the table and leaned forward conspiratorially. "Have you ever kissed a girl?" she asked in a low voice.

"What?" Jenny absently tapped her highlighter against her cheek, apparently forgetting the top was off, leaving a tiny yellow splotch near the corner of her mouth. She looked a little bewildered. "I don't know. You mean, like . . . seriously? Or like you and Kara at the meeting the other night?"

"Well . . ." Brett glanced around them, suddenly feeling paranoid. Was that guy from her calc class over there eavesdropping? No, he had tiny white earphones stuck in his ears. "The thing is, we sort of did it again." Brett twisted the gold chain of her pendant necklace around her index finger. "Last night."

"Wait, *what*?" Jenny looked like she'd suddenly been hit with a bucket of ice-cold water. "You mean, like, made out?" Her voice squealed a little on the last two words.

"Shhhh!" Brett pressed her finger to her lips. She didn't want to shock the two older women to her left. Although in their long, shapeless patterned dresses, they could be lesbians themselves. But wait—you couldn't tell a person's sexuality just by *looking* at them, she reminded herself. That was exactly what she didn't want other people to be doing to *her*. She put her elbows on the table, forgetting that the delicate silk fabric of her Anna Sui peasant blouse would probably stick to the leftover coffee goo. "I don't know. Sort of. I mean . . . I really have no idea what it was."

"Ohmigod." Jenny made a steeple with her fingers and tapped them rapidly against each other. "That is so crazy. What was it like?"

Brett felt a rush of warmth for Jenny. She had responded totally perfectly—surprised and curious, of course, but not shocked or horrified. Brett never would have been able to tell something like this to Tinsley—even back in the day, when they were allegedly friends—without Tinsley making a snide comment about Brett needing to buy a pair of butch Birkenstocks or something like that. "It was . . . nice," she admitted, shrugging her shoulders. "But I'm just so confused, you know?"

"I can imagine." Jenny took a sip from her navy blue coffee mug with the words MIKE'S AUTOMOTIVE on the side. The CoffeeRoasters owners allegedly bought their mismatched dishes and mugs at yard sales. The idea was sort of charming, actually. "So . . . do you, like, want to do it again?"

Brett's face flushed. "Kind of." Meaning, yeah. She paused, eyeing Jenny's face. "Do you think that's weird?"

"I doubt you're the first person in the world to kiss a girl and like it." Jenny giggled. The cappuccino machine whirred to life over Brett's shoulder, hissing loudly. "I mean, girls are beautiful. Why wouldn't you want to kiss them? Girls always smell nice, and boys can be totally grody sometimes." Then her face turned a little more serious. "And Kara is awesome. She's cute and sweet and fun to be around."

Brett felt herself start to blush. Was she really thinking about Kara like that? Well, she guessed so. Even though she'd been a little embarrassed to start the conversation, she had to admit it felt good to get it all off her chest. As confused as she was, she was excited, too, and it was nice to get to talk about it with Jenny. "So, I must be bi, then, right?" Brett continued, lowering her voice. "Or is this just some sort of reaction to getting screwed over one too many times by a jackass guy?"

Jenny swallowed a gulp of coffee. She peered over her mug thoughtfully. "I don't know. You've had a few big, I don't know, *crashes* lately." She traced her thumb along the rim of her cup before tearing open another packet of Splenda and emptying it into her drink. "But maybe it's a good idea to not try and label things yet, you know? Labels don't really mean anything."

Brett pressed her lips together in a slight pout. "But I like labels," she admitted. "They make everything so much clearer." Her sister Bree always told her she liked things to be wrapped up too neatly, and that part of the point of life was its messiness, its refusal to be wrapped up. Brett always took the advice with a grain of salt—it was probably Bree's excuse for a messy room, or for breaking up with boys she'd dated *without actually telling them*. But maybe Jenny had a point?

Jenny tilted her head sympathetically. "You don't need to overanalyze everything. Just . . . follow your heart. And don't worry—your secret's safe with me." She brought a dainty finger up to her mouth and pretended to zip her lips.

Brett nodded slightly. Follow her heart. Right. How many times had she been told to do that, and where had it led her so far? To its being broken *twice* in the past month and a half. But still. Kara was about as different from Eric Dalton and Jeremiah Mortimer as you could get—personality-wise as well as anatomically. Not that she knew much about Kara's anatomy. At least, not yet.

23

A LITTLE HEALTHY COMPETITION IS GOOD FOR

AN OWL.

"You suck, Buchanan," Julian spat as he threw his tall body across the blond wood squash court in a feeble effort to return the perfectly placed drop shot Brandon had just unloaded. He crashed into the smudged white wall of the court as the ball dropped harmlessly in front of him.

"How come I just kicked your ass then?" Brandon let his racquet clatter to the ground and stretched a sweaty hand out to where Julian was sprawled, panting, on the floor. Julian took it and stood up with a groan. On the other courts the thwacking sounds of squash balls hitting racquets, walls, and sweaty boys continued, but Brandon had just beaten Julian, the second-best player on the team, for the fourth game in the row. It was one of the best feelings in the world when everything about his game seemed to be working for him—when his reflexes were instantaneous, when his shots were all slapped at exactly the right angle, when he could almost tell where the ball was going to land even before his opponent hit it. He was just . . . *on*. Maybe it had something to do with the sexy text message he'd gotten from Elizabeth right before practice?

"Yeah, whatever." Julian shook Brandon's hand good-naturedly before wiping his once-white wristband against his glistening forehead. "Just wait until next time."

"Do you think maybe your incredible losing streak to me may have something to do with that girly thing on your head?" Brandon gestured toward Julian's ponytail. Was the Tom-Cruise-in-*Magnolia* look ever a good idea? Was any Tom Cruise look *ever* a good idea? Brandon pushed open the court door and started to head toward the water fountain.

"Nice game, sexy." Startled, Brandon looked up toward the three benches that served as bleachers (there were never that many spectators for squash games) and noticed Elizabeth sitting on the middle one, wearing a denim miniskirt that looked like she had cut it off herself, black tights, and a scoop-neck black leotard top. The heels of her mid-calf Doc Martens were perched almost delicately on the edge of the bench below her. Her dirty blond hair spilled across her shoulders as she pulled her white earphones out of her silver-studded ears.

Brandon hadn't realized he was staring at her until Julian nudged him in the ribs. "*Hey*." Brandon started over to her, still a little astonished at the sight of her somewhere as banal as the squash courts. It was almost as if he had conjured her up, since he'd been thinking about her nonstop since their make-out session in her room yesterday. She was just so hot, and sweet. And funny, and— "What are you doing here?" Brandon asked, suddenly self-conscious of the fact that he was practically dripping with sweat. He swiped his wristband across his face quickly.

"Watching you wipe the floor with that poor kid." Her brown eyes twinkled amusedly as Brandon slid toward her on the bleacher.

He swelled with pride but was grateful he hadn't noticed Elizabeth—and her sexy legs—sooner, as it probably would have distracted him. Callie had come to watch him play in one of the big tournaments once, and Brandon had been so self-conscious the entire time he'd gotten completely crushed by this kid from Deerfield whom he'd destroyed the last five times they'd played, much to the detriment of his masculine pride. Callie had tried to cheer him up afterward, telling him it hadn't been so bad, but Brandon could detect the hint of disappointment in her pretty face—and he could almost hear her control-freak mother chiding, "Vernons do not date losers." Callie had actually canceled their plans for that night, saying she'd forgotten that it was the season finale of *America's Next Top Model*. He decided to take it as a good omen that his and Elizabeth's relationship was starting off on the right foot.

"Thanks. You're looking pretty good yourself, you know."

"And I'm just sitting here." Elizabeth winked at him. "So, uh, is your practice over? Can you hang out?"

Before he could answer, Brian Atherton, a senior who called everyone on the team "dude" and who shaved his head in a vain attempt to disguise his premature balding, threw an arm around Brandon's shoulders as if they were best friends instead of just reluctantly civil teammates. "Dude," Atherton intoned, his mouth practically hanging open at the sight of Elizabeth, "this your girlfriend?"

Brandon noticed suddenly that the courts were noticeably quieter, no longer ringing with the sounds of cursing boys or of racquets clattering against the walls. Brandon casually eased himself out from under Atherton's weighty arm and replied without really thinking about it. "Yeah. This is Elizabeth." He tilted his head toward Atherton. "This is Atherton."

Atherton propped one of his sneakers up on the lowest bench and pretended to stretch out his calf muscle. "So how come you're with this kid?" he asked incredulously, his eyes greedily taking in her partly bare shoulders as he squeezed his water bottle into his mouth. Brandon had seen him stare that exact same way at a Big Mac after an away match once. Disgusting.

Elizabeth stared straight back at Atherton, apparently unimpressed. She shrugged and smiled, the dimple beneath her lips deepening impishly. Brandon caught her eye and could tell something was wrong. He quickly shoved Atherton aside and swooped her out the door.

"You okay?" Brandon asked, once the heavy doors of the squash complex clicked shut behind them. The cool air felt good on his hot skin as he stuffed his wristbands into the outer pocket of his black vinyl squash bag. "Sorry about Atherton. He's kind of an ass." He looked down and realized he was still wearing his court sneakers. They were technically not supposed to be worn outside the courts—the squash complex was a new, expensive addition to Waverly, and there were threatening signs posted everywhere.

"Yeah." Elizabeth touched her hair distractedly and tugged on her leather bomber jacket. She zipped it up, shutting off Brandon's view of that insanely enticing collarbone. "Um, you're really special to me. . . ." *Uh-oh.* He turned to face her. She hadn't come all the way over to break up with him, had she? "But . . . just the word 'girlfriend' sort of made me cringe, you know?" She bit her lip.

"Um, okay . . ." Brandon had no idea what was happening. He wasn't even the one who had used the term "girlfriend"— but that was kind of what she was, wasn't she? Except . . . now she was saying she didn't want to be?

Elizabeth placed a hand on his bare arm, and he stared down wordlessly at her pale pink nails as she squeezed him gently. She had no business touching him like that if she was breaking up with him.

And yet, she didn't move her hand away. In fact, she started stroking her thumb against his wrist, and Brandon had to try really hard not to get completely turned on. "So, what are you saying, exactly?" he asked, sort of awkwardly.

"I'm just saying I need to be kind of, you know, *open* about these things." Her brown eyes stared up at him through their thick, dark web of lashes. "I just hate to feel . . . trapped?" Her eyes searched his, looking for understanding.

Wait, what? So, she wasn't breaking up with him—she was just saying she wanted to um, *study*, with other people?

"What do you think about that?" Elizabeth whispered, scooting a little closer toward him so that the honey-and-incense smell of her hair sent him reeling back to yesterday afternoon in her room.

And suddenly, Brandon wasn't exactly thinking.

 **Owl** Net

To: Women of Waverly; HeathFerro@waverly.edu
From: KaraWhalen@waverly.edu
Date: Thursday, October 10, 1:15 P.M.
Subject: Women of Waverly meeting

Ladies (and Heath),

The second official WoW meeting will be held tonight at 7 P.M. The atrium is booked, so we can all meet in my room (Dumbarton 107) if you don't mind cramming in!

Thanks for making the first one such a success—spread the word about tonight, and don't be afraid to bring your questions! Tonight's topic is LOVE.

Heath—you're welcome to come, but, as it'll be after visitation hours, don't get caught.

xo,

Kara

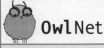

OwlNet   Email Inbox

To: KaraWhalen@waverly.edu; Women of Waverly
From: HeathFerro@waverly.edu
Date: Thursday, October 10, 4:51 P.M.
Subject: Re: Women of Waverly meeting

Have no fear, my dears—I will come bearing gifts for my fellow girls!!

xxx,

H.F.

OwlNet   Email Inbox

To: Julian McCafferty@waverly.edu
From: TinsleyCarmichael@waverly.edu
Date: Thursday, October 10, 4:59 P.M.
Subject: Signal

Not sure what happened to you yesterday, but it's your lucky day—I'm giving you a second chance. Don't stand me up again or you'll be sorry.

Kisses!

T

25

A WAVERLY OWL MUST GIVE A LITTLE TO GET A LITTLE.

Brett dropped the last of the beanbags from the upstairs lounge area onto Kara's dorm room floor and straightened, lightly massaging her shoulder with her hand. In preparation for the Women of Waverly meeting, they'd dragged a half-dozen of the lumpy things from the lounge and somehow squeezed them all into the now-tight space, so the room was a sea of huge, brightly colored vinyl balls. Kara flopped down into a dark blue beanbag chair. Brett had always hated the things—except now they seemed kind of, well, sexy. Hesitating only slightly, she sat down next to Kara, her body weight bobbling the two of them a bit, and making them giggle. Talking with Jenny this afternoon had made Brett feel more comfortable about the whole thing. Not that she'd been feeling *uncomfortable*, exactly, but still.

"What are we going to talk about at the meeting tonight?"

Brett asked, conscious of the fact that their arms were touching. She felt the filler in the beanbag shift a little, and she sank even closer to Kara so that their legs were touching too.

Kara twisted her silver chain necklace so that the clasp ended up back where it belonged. Her nails were painted a pale pink, a color that made Brett think of her own Pinkie Swear Crazy Daisy, and chipped at the ends. She had on no other makeup, and she didn't need it. She had tiny, pale freckles sprinkled across the tops of her cheeks, so faint you only noticed them when you were really close to her. Like Brett was now. "The theme is love, so maybe we could talk about different kinds of love?" Kara suggested, her eyebrows delicately arched.

"Um . . ." But Brett couldn't think about anything but kissing Kara again, and before saying anything else, she leaned in toward her. Kara obviously wasn't shocked, and her lips moved instinctively against Brett's, sending shivers down her spine. She tried not to compare kissing Kara to kissing Jeremiah, but she couldn't help it—it was like she'd been eating apples all her life, and now she'd tried brussels sprouts after a lifetime of thinking she hated them, only to find that they were sweeter than sugar. Kara's lips were just so soft. And she was an excellent kisser. Brett's hand rose to touch Kara's cheek.

"Ta-da!!!"

The girls pulled apart, surprised, and turned to find Heath Ferro standing in Kara's doorway, in . . . drag. He had on a long, dirty blond wig and enormous brown-tinted Gucci sunglasses, which he pulled off his face the second he saw the two girls entwined. "Holy fucking shit!"

Brett leapt to her feet first, her face on fire. "Close the door, asshole," she hissed at him but then sprang toward it and closed it herself. "What the hell are you doing here?"

Heath clasped his hands to his mouth. His eyes were all bugged out with excitement, and if the situation hadn't been so serious, Brett probably would have laughed at the fact that he kind of did look like a girl in that wig—a pretty one, even. He wasn't dressed like a girl, though, wearing a pair of beat-up khakis and a tight black T-shirt that clearly revealed his lack of breasts. But maybe at first glance, someone might take him for one. "Don't let me interrupt you, please. That was, like, the hottest thing I have ever seen!"

"Heath, you can*not* tell anyone about this." Brett pressed her hands to her temples, meeting Kara's equally panicked eyes across the room. "I am *serious*. You have to swear, okay?" Crazily, even in her freaked-out state Brett couldn't help but notice how pretty Kara looked when she was scared.

Heath tucked the sunglasses absentmindedly into his shirt collar, an elated smile still spread across his face. He looked like he had just walked into the Playboy Mansion. "I promise— really, I swear to everything I have ever loved—I won't tell anyone about this. Ever." He looked at the two girls earnestly and then fumbled through his backpack for something, at last pulling out . . . a digital camera. "As long as I can have one picture?"

"What?" Brett pressed her lips together, annoyed. But as she looked at Heath's eager, kid-in-a-candy-store face, she began to sense that he didn't pose a real threat after all—at least, not as long as he was kept amused. Brett tapped the toe of her tan suede Campers against the polished wood floor.

"No fucking way." Kara shook her head at Heath from her seat on the beanbag, leaning back. She smoothed out her short black skirt, and Brett could feel Heath watching her intently, to see if *she* was looking at Kara's legs. Boys.

"Come on, one little picture. That's all I'm asking, in exchange for keeping your secret." Heath glanced back and forth between the girls, absentmindedly tugging the hair of his blond wig. "Puh-lease? You guys are so fucking hot together."

Brett finally caught Kara's eyes and tried to send her a message with her own. *Just follow my lead,* she tried to say. "Well . . ." Brett rubbed her chin between her thumb and forefinger. "Maybe just one." If that was all it took to keep Heath Ferro's mouth shut, it really wasn't a high price to pay.

"Oh my God, I love you guys." Heath giddily turned on his tiny silver Nokia, his hair hanging crookedly off his head, and Brett gave Kara a wink.

Kara grinned and stood up, stretching her limbs. She strode over to where Brett was standing and touched her on the arm. "Ready?" she asked, her eyebrows raised. *Are you sure?* her eyes seemed to say.

"Yup," Brett giggled, pushing a loose strand of hair behind her left ear. And their faces moved toward each other slowly, as if they were in a movie, their lips meeting and opening softly against each other. It was kind of . . . sexy to have someone watch them. It wasn't like before, when they were alone, but it was exciting in a different way, almost like letting someone else in on their secret had made it that much more electrifying. She pulled away reluctantly.

"How was that?" Brett turned to Heath, her hand perched defiantly on her hip.

He ran his hand across his scalp, forgetting it wasn't his own. The wig slid to the left, so that the dirty blond hair was perched crookedly on his head. "Is this heaven? Because . . . someone up there really loves me." He stared at the tiny screen on his camera and clicked through the pictures.

"Let me see how they turned out." Kara grabbed the camera from his hands and held it out so Brett could see. Heath had taken about ten pictures of them in the five seconds they had been kissing, and Brett watched images of herself and Kara flick up on the tiny screen. She had to admit, they *were* kind of hot together. After scrolling through them all once, Kara quickly started to delete them.

"Hey, what are you doing?" Heath grabbed for his camera. "You said I could have one!" He lunged after Kara, but Brett held him back until she could finish. Kara hopped onto her bed and stood there, deleting all the saved photos. "*No!*" he wailed, actually kind of sounding like a girl. Which was sort of fitting, considering that he looked like one.

Brett patted Heath's back. "Listen. How about this? Every day that you keep this a secret, we'll take a sexy photo together and e-mail it to you. Okay?" She glanced at Kara, who was still standing on top of her bed, barefoot in her tights.

"So for now," Kara continued, bouncing on her toes, framed

by a black-and-white poster of a young Bob Dylan above her bed, "the camera is ours."

"If you send me secret sexy pictures, just for myself"— Heath gulped, as if breathless at the thought—"I promise I will take your secret to my grave." He put a hand over his heart.

"Deal." Brett's heart-shaped lips curled into a grin, and she met Kara's eyes once again. "You understand, of course," she lowered her voice to her most threatening register possible, "that if this gets out—we'll have to kill you."

"Oh, I promise," Heath said, pressing his hands together as if he were praying. "I really, really promise. I swear on all that is holy." His normally lazy-looking green eyes were flashing with—what? Was that sincerity?

Or just pure lust?

A WAVERLY OWL KNOWS THAT SOMETIMES HARD WORK IS THE BEST MEDICINE.

Jenny set down her art supplies on a table in the center of the studio, and the heavy box of pastels clanged against the metal, resounding in the enormous, totally empty space. The building was open most evenings for anyone who needed more time at the sketching tables, but most students didn't take advantage of it.

She turned on Mrs. Silver's boom box to keep her company. It was tuned to some oldies station, but Jenny left it there—it kind of made her think of her dad, and how every morning he'd shuffle around the kitchen in his slippers, making coffee to one of the three Beatles CDs he kept in regular rotation on the portable CD player Jenny and Dan had bought him for Christmas. "Oldies for the oldie," he liked to say.

As she came back to her desk and began to arrange her art supplies into neat categories, Jenny couldn't help but smile.

She loved the art building when no one else was around. The huge plate glass windows looked out on the brightly colored leaves, tinges of which were still visible even though the sun was just setting, and the reflections of the track lights twinkled back at her. The windows reminded her a little of the city, of walking down Columbus Avenue at night and looking into the enormous shop windows, the people walking on the street reflected inside them.

Jenny looked up as the studio door clattered open and Julian stepped inside, chewing on an apple. She could see the dimple next to his mouth. She grinned from across the giant room.

"Hey there." Her voice echoed across the empty studio, carrying over the sound of an old Rolling Stones song. She waved Julian over toward where she was setting out her supplies: a giant block of watercolor paper, pastels, charcoals, watercolors, even a few tubes of paint. She'd come overprepared because she wasn't sure what medium she wanted to use, exactly. She was sort of waiting for . . . inspiration. "You made it," she added with a smile.

Julian took another chomp of his green apple and took in the high, sloping ceilings and the huge dramatic windows appreciatively. Then his eyes trailed down to her and his golden brown eyes widened. "Hey, am I dressed okay for this? I know you love the T-shirts, but . . ." His shaggy brownish-blondish hair was loose and he was wearing a long-sleeve button down beneath a tight-fitting Raconteurs concert T-shirt and a pair of black cuffed dress pants. "I mean, *you* look really nice. Like someone should be drawing you," he added.

Jenny willed herself not to blush at the compliment. She had been surprisingly nervous getting ready but had finally decided on her chocolate brown Free People puff-sleeve mock turtleneck made of something super-soft that looked silky in the light, and a pair of dark fitted jeans from the Gap that she'd had forever. Definitely nothing fancy, but it was totally sweet of Julian to tell her she looked nice. She *had* dusted her eyelids with a little Bare Escentuals Eye Glimmer in Fire Light. "Um, thanks. But yeah—you're dressed fine," she finally answered, hoping she hadn't blushed in spite of herself.

"Cool." Julian hopped up onto the little mini-stage in the middle of the studio, where the models posed during class. His heavy hiking boots clomped loudly against the wooden platform, and with the extra height he towered over Jenny—even more than usual. "Is this where you want me?" he asked with a grin.

"Maybe . . ." Jenny rubbed her thumb against her chin, as she always did when she was trying to picture her composition. Julian was so tall and gangly—she felt like his portrait should somehow capture that. "Um, what about the chair?" She motioned over to the worn-out velvet armchair that had randomly appeared in the art studio the other day. The theater department had donated it to the art department, and Mrs. Silver had immediately commandeered it for the models to pose on, in her continual search for furniture that was "inspiring." It was kind of saggy, and the fabric was worn through to bare canvas at some points, but enough of the royal-blue-striped velvet covered the chair to make it seem somehow regal and exciting, like their own personal throne. Julian, King of the . . . what? Very tall, very cute people?

Julian sank into the chair, which suddenly looked small, his knees practically coming up to his chest. Jenny couldn't help giggling. He coughed and stretched out, yawning, extending his long legs and sinking back into the chair. "I feel like this chair is eating me alive."

"Are you comfortable?" Jenny asked, her pencil already flying across her paper. "That's a great pose—it really captures how tall you are."

Julian shifted a little in the chair. He looked like a basketball player trying to get comfortable in a piece of dollhouse furniture. "S'all right. As long as I don't have to stay here forever."

"I'll work fast," Jenny promised—although she was thinking about how nice it felt to be here with Julian, and she kind of wished she didn't ever have to leave and go back out into reality. The art studio had to be her favorite building on campus, and Julian took her mind off Easy. And right now, the last thing in the world she wanted to think about was Easy Walsh, and how he was the last guy whose portrait she'd drawn. And how he'd drawn her, in the woods. Maybe drawing someone was a relationship death sentence, like poking a voodoo doll with pins.

Her pencil hovered midstroke over the thick white paper. Was she totally imagining the chemistry she felt with Julian? She couldn't help remembering the way she'd been certain—completely, never-been-more-sure-of-anything-in-her-life certain—that there was something between her and Easy, something real. And then, almost as quickly as it had started, it fizzled out. As sad as she was about losing Easy, she was sadder about the fact that she had so completely misjudged things. "Love is not love which alters when it alteration finds, or bends with the remover to remove." Or so said Shakespeare, who seemed to know a thing or two about it. Part of her had thought she'd crumble if she and Easy broke up—yet here she was, days later, already fantasizing about being stranded on a tropical island with someone else.

Julian swallowed a big chunk of apple, hardly pausing to chew. "I've never been in here before." His eyes wandered across the high angled ceilings and the huge walls of windows.

"Sometimes I like to pretend I'm some famous artist and this is my SoHo loft." Jenny stepped back from her angled desk to look at her preliminary drawing. She'd sketched in Julian's figure, crouched somehow both awkwardly and elegantly in the armchair. The sleek lines of the graphite seemed to suit him well as a subject—if she were to change to another medium, she'd definitely lose some of the immediacy of him she thought she was capturing. The scene gave her the feeling that it could disappear at any moment: Julian could stand up and stretch out and walk away. The spontaneity of pencil just seemed right for him.

He looked right at Jenny, sending a little jolt through her, like when she was in a hurry and only had time for an espresso shot in the morning. "Except you can see trees outside."

She tried to capture Julian's sagging shoulders, the relaxed posture of his body that seemed to contrast with his almost uncapturable energy. "They have trees in the city, you know."

"Oh, yeah?" He lifted his chin at her. "Like, five."

"Ever heard of Central Park?" Jenny asked incredulously, trying not to smile. Her pencil soared across the paper. "It's, like, nine hundred acres of trees."

Julian chuckled and shook his head. "Don't get defensive. I just like my cities with trees."

"Are you going to start bashing New York? Because I don't think I can draw anyone who doesn't realize it's the greatest city on the planet." Jenny paused, lifting her pencil from the paper threateningly. "I mean, that would just go against everything I believe in," she said playfully.

"Well, I kind of already told my mom I was getting my portrait done. So I'd better not screw it up now."

"How could I disappoint someone's mother?" Jenny sighed with mock resignation and returned to her drawing. How adorable was it that he'd told his mom about their portrait session? "You really do have a great face, you know," she couldn't help adding. It was true. After sketching in the framework of the drawing, Jenny finally was able to concentrate on the part she'd been trying hard to avoid staring at: Julian's face. "Very expressive."

"Girls like the broken nose," he said a little shyly. "It makes them think I'm tough."

Jenny blew a stray hair out of her eyes. "Are you?"

"Depends on your definition."

"I think being tough means . . ." She held her pencil away from the paper for a minute to think. She could feel his eyes scanning her face. "Means not being afraid to make a fool of yourself."

"Then I'm Rambo and the Terminator rolled into one." Julian laughed. "I've been known to make a fool of myself more than once, and have a good time doing it." He had a great, goofy laugh—it made his mouth open so wide you could practically tell whether he'd had his tonsils out. Immediately, she tore off the top sheet of her pad of paper and started a new sketch. She *had* to draw his laugh—the way it made his whole body shake with energy, with delight, with pure pleasure in being exactly where he was, at exactly that moment. Jenny could read it all in his body language, and she was determined to try and capture it on paper. She thought again about the assignment Mrs. Silver had given them: to reveal something about the subject's personality. She wanted everyone to look at her portrait of Julian and think, *Yeah, that is totally what that kid is like!*

"Um, would you mind if I drew you while you're laughing?" Jenny asked, a little tentatively. "I mean, you don't have to be laughing the whole time or anything—but if you could keep trying, that would be great?"

"First you want to me to sit in that baby-bear chair, and now you want me to pose laughing?" Julian stared at her incredulously, looking amused nonetheless. "You didn't tell me this was going to be *hard*." And then he laughed again, and Jenny's pencil flitted across the paper. "You're going to have to tell me some good jokes."

She groaned. "I'm really horrible at jokes. I always ruin them."

"Well," Julian teased, "if being tough means not being afraid to make a fool of yourself . . ."

A giggle came bursting out of Jenny's throat. His energy was infectious. "All right," she said, her brain searching way back into its recesses for the sort of witty, creative joke that might impress Julian. Nothing. "Okay . . . Knock, knock."

He burst out laughing, and the sounds of the two of them seemed to rise up to the ceiling and fill the entire room.

Time passed like nothing at all, and it wasn't until Julian had to get up and stretch for the fourth time, and made his millionth adorable, funny face for Jenny's amusement, that she realized, with a shock, that she had completely missed the Women of Waverly meeting.

 **Owl**Net

From: TinsleyCarmichael@waverly.edu
To: JulianMcCafferty@waverly.edu
Date: Thursday, October 10, 8:55 P.M.
Subject: Uh, hello?

J,

Did you get my e-mail? Playing hard to get? Well, fine. It's working. . . .

T

A WAVERLY OWL KNOWS THAT JUICY SECRETS ARE MEANT TO BE SHARED.

Callie yawned and tried to psych herself up to get out of her cozy beanbag, but the vodka she'd drunk during the WoW meeting had made her limbs heavy, and she quickly gave up. Heath had, as promised, come bearing gifts—in this case, three bottles of Stoli, wrapped up snugly in sweatshirts in his backpack. Much to the delight of the ladies, he had worn a long blond wig and told everyone he was the new Swedish exchange student, Inga. There was always something bizarre about football guys using Halloween as an excuse to wear cheerleader outfits and stuff balloons up their sweaters, but Heath had been a natural Inga, in his normal boy clothes and gorgeous head of long, silky blond hair that he kept stroking throughout the meeting. At 9:10, just before Pardee generally started doing her pre-curfew rounds, the Women of Waverly meeting disbanded, the girls rising reluctantly from their cushy beanbags.

"Ladies." Heath bowed graciously, the hair of his wig almost touching the ground. "It has been a real pleasure."

"Looks clear." Brett had her entire torso stuck out Kara's open window. She pulled herself back in and took another sip from her not-just-Arizona iced tea. "You should get out of here." To everyone's surprise, she gave him a quick, drunken hug before unceremoniously shoving him toward the window. Callie raised an eyebrow. Since when did Brett Messerschmidt deign to touch sleazy Heath Ferro?

Once Kara closed the window behind him, the other girls started to trickle out the door, still buzzing with excitement and a little tipsy. The discussion topic for the night had been love, and everyone had something to say about it, especially when their tongues were loosened by Heath's vodka. But for most of the meeting, Callie had just nestled into her beanbag and nursed her spiked Country Time lemonade. It was great that Rifat and Benny and Sage could all talk about their crushes and loves and heartbreaks and all, but Callie wasn't exactly in a position to share what was happening with *her*, no matter how relevant her current goings-on were to the subject at hand.

"Coming, babe?" Benny kicked her socked toe into Callie's beanbag and giggled, her thick, perfectly shiny brown hair neatly in place behind her small, diamond-studded ears. Even when Benny was drunk, she never managed to look it. Apparently that was one of the genetic benefits of being practically descended from aristocracy. "You need to get upstairs and dry out."

Callie sighed heavily and started to get to her feet, but

the room immediately started spinning like an evil merry-go-round, and she sank back into her seat. She rested the back of her hand over her eyes and wished everyone would just go away. She peeked through her fingers to see if Benny was going to bug her more, but she was already headed for the door. Callie couldn't help feeling a little sorry for her dizzy, helpless self. Brett and Kara were standing at the door, their heads together, whispering. Great. They were probably complaining about her drunkenness, how they were stuck with her. Bitches. But then Brett gave her a smile that looked sincere and disappeared out the door.

Callie sniffled miserably and noticed for the first time a run in the knee of her dove gray nylons. "Fuck." She fingered the snag, wondering if she'd gotten it from sitting on that stinking hay in the stables. An almost unbearable wave of longing washed over her as she thought about how just a few hours ago she had been alone with Easy, and she'd only let him kiss her as they said goodbye. It had taken an almost unprecedented amount of self-control on her part, and she knew that if he were in front of her right now, she'd throw herself at him and devour him with kisses. Why the fuck had she been holding out for so long? He was in love with her—finally. And she loved him. "Why does anything else have to matter?"

"What?" Kara, who had been stooping down to pick up an empty Dixie cup off the floor, stood up and looked at Callie quizzically, her round cheeks flushed pink with alcohol. Callie certainly hadn't realized she'd spoken out loud, but once she did, it was like the seal was broken. Although her tongue moved slowly in her mouth, she couldn't stop it.

Callie re-crossed her legs so that she couldn't see the snag anymore. "You know. Why isn't love ever enough? Like, why do other things matter so much?"

Kara nodded her head slowly. Callie felt a touch of warmth for Kara for not staring at her like she was insane, instead ignoring the probably drunken sound of her voice and listening to her words. That was sweet. She was sweet. "What do you mean? What other things?" Kara asked.

"You know," Callie repeated, leaning back into her chair, enjoying the noise the little beans—or whatever the hell was inside—made as they shifted to accommodate her. *That's more like it,* she thought drunkenly. "All the hiding your real feelings . . . and sneaking around. Just so people don't get hurt . . . when all you want to do is just be in love." She felt herself waving her arms about her, but they seemed to be doing it on their own, without any sort of signal from her brain.

Kara flopped into a chair next to Callie and put her elbows on her knees. She was wearing a flattering chocolate-colored tunic with bell sleeves over a short black skirt and black tights. It wasn't really a look Callie would go for herself, but it seemed to suit Kara well. She took a swig of her own drink. "Wait, so what exactly are you talking about?"

Callie pushed a tangled piece of hair back from her face. "Um, you kind of have to swear not to tell anyone, okay?"

Kara's friendly greeny-brown eyes seemed to smile at her as she nodded solemnly. She reminded Callie a little of a girl who had been her best friend way back in the second grade. Alena something. Yeah, Alena was nice. "I swear."

Callie lowered her chin a little, her head starting to feel heavy. "Well . . . Easy and I are sort of seeing each other again."

Kara's mouth formed a little *O* of surprise. "Oh, wow." She exhaled loudly. She crossed her ankles and Callie caught a glimpse of her anklet—a tiny, worn-out leather strap with a peace-sign pendant on it.

"I mean, I know it's really shitty," Callie continued quickly. "Because of the promise I made to Jenny and all . . . which I really meant to keep." She dug her long nails into her scalp. "But it's just too hard. I still love him. Am I supposed to, you know, fight it? Forever?"

She pictured herself as a glamorous thirtysomething interior designer or big-shot editor in the city, owning her own swanky uptown apartment and having weekly salons and soirees where exotic and brilliant movie stars and writers and artists came to get drunk and flirt. Then one day, raggedy starving-artist Easy would turn up on her doorstep and tell her he still loved her. And she was supposed to turn him away even then? It just wasn't fair.

"No," Kara answered emphatically, surprising Callie. She wasn't sure why she was sharing this with Kara, when Kara and Jenny were kind of buddy-buddy. But something about Kara—maybe the way she looked kind of tortured herself?—had compelled Callie to open up. That and the vodka. Obviously. "I mean, you have to be a little sensitive, of course, because there are a lot of people involved." She shrugged her petite shoulders. "But if you're in love . . . that's out of your control, right? We don't get to pick the people we fall in love with. And it's really nothing to be ashamed of, is it?"

"Not at all." Callie nodded. She raised her iced tea bottle toward her and they drunkenly clinked glasses, both giggling. "There aren't that many real things in this world, you know? And love is one of them," she slurred, sounding like a cheesy pop song—or a prolific stoner.

"You know . . ." Kara cleared her throat after sipping her drink. "I'm kind of . . . seeing someone in secret too."

It was Callie's turn to be shocked. "Just tell me it's not Heath Ferro, okay?" Heath had sat next to Kara all night, kind of staring at her with his googly eyes, like he was picturing her naked. Because if she had to listen to Kara talk about being in love with skeezoid Heath, she'd probably vomit. Which, admittedly, she'd probably be doing pretty soon anyway.

Kara laughed. "It's not Heath. But you'll promise not to tell anyone either, okay? I mean, it would be really . . . weird if this got out."

Callie nodded as emphatically as she could in her drunken state. Her stomach was already started to gurgle, and she knew—unfortunately—from experience that once you started thinking about vomiting, that meant it wasn't too far in the future.

"It's, uh . . . Brett."

WOW! was right.

28

A FORMER ENEMY CAN OFTEN BE AN OWL'S MOST VALUABLE ALLY.

Brandon hesitated outside the door of Easy Walsh's room, not quite confident he should be doing this. He hated Walsh with a passion—the way he'd swept in like a vulture last year and stolen Callie away from him, and then the way he'd tossed Callie aside as soon as funky, cute little Jenny Humphrey came along, and the way he was tossing Jenny aside right now. He hated everything about him, including the way his jeans were always just *so perfectly* splattered with paint, so as to remind everyone in the entire world that he was an *artist*. Everything about him was just so fucking effortless—and it drove Brandon absolutely insane.

And yet, they'd had sort of a cease-fire moment when Brandon bumped into him in the woods earlier in the week. Walsh had actually asked for his advice—like he wasn't even aware of the fact that Brandon was waiting for the day when he got expelled so that he could gleefully wave goodbye to him forever. If Walsh could be big about it and ask for Brandon's opinion on something, then, well, Brandon wasn't going to let him be the only mature one. Resolutely, he knocked on the door.

"Yeah?" a muffled voice called out from the inside, distractedly. Brandon opened the door and stood in the doorway awkwardly. Easy was lying on his back on his unmade bed, hands cupped under his head, staring at the ceiling. Brandon reflexively glanced up to see if maybe there was something there—a dirty poster, or maybe some of those glow-in-the-dark star stickers, but there was nothing.

"Hey." Brandon coughed. "You busy?"

"Dude, do I look busy?"

Brandon bristled, but then Easy turned his head slightly and gave him a half-grin. If he was surprised to see him there, his face showed no sign of it. Thankfully, Easy's pothead roommate, Alan St. Girard, was off somewhere, probably making out with his new girlfriend, Alison Quentin, who was also way too good for him.

"Hey, everyone works in different ways." Brandon shrugged, trying to look as casual as Easy.

"Definitely not working." Easy rolled onto his side, propping himself up on one elbow. He had on his requisite paint-covered jeans and a T-shirt that looked like it had once—a long, long time ago—been white. Bob Dylan's harmonica was screeching out of the white iPod docking station. "What's up?"

"I don't know." Brandon picked up a notebook off a desk chair and placed it gingerly on the overflowing desk, then sat down. This was totally awkward. He was going to ask Walsh for girl advice? "This . . . girl. She's driving me nuts."

Easy nodded slowly. "The one at the party? Leather jacket? Free Tibet?"

Brandon felt his chest puff up with pride. "Yeah, Elizabeth. She's awesome, but she's sort of hard to get, you know?" Brandon played with the French cuff of his navy pin-striped Banana Republic dress shirt. "The thing is, she's kind of like you—she's like a, you know, *free spirit*. Doesn't-want-to-be-tied-down kind of thing."

"So you want my advice?" Easy rubbed his neck, sounding a little surprised.

Brandon bit the inside of his cheek. "Uh, yeah. I like her. I want to be with her. I don't want to chase her away or anything, though."

"Well, if she's like me, then you've got to just let her be who she is." Easy sat up and swung his feet to the floor. Both his white socks had giant holes in the toes. Didn't his parents give him packages of new socks for Christmas like everyone else's? Even if they didn't—was it so hard to buy them yourself?

Brandon tore his eyes away from Easy's socks. He scanned the room, counting five paper coffee cups from Maxwell Hall— he recognized them from the little maroon owl on the white background. Either Easy or his roommate had a coffee problem. And both of them had a cleanliness problem. He tried to focus on what Easy was saying. "I definitely don't want her to not be who she is—I just want to be with her as she, you know, *is* who she is."

"That's cool then. It sounds like you just have to, like, be chill. Don't push. People like us get all defensive when other people try to change us." Easy yawned hugely, revealing the two platinum fillings in his molars. "But then, once you're in love, even if they're like me or Elizabeth or whoever, people can be willing to change. You've just got to get there first."

Brandon nodded his head slowly. "That actually makes sense." This was definitely the longest conversation with Walsh that Brandon had ever had. Maybe he wasn't such a horrible person after all. He seemed cool enough, willing to help him out. Maybe he was just better at giving advice about girls than following it himself. "I'm going to give her so much space to be herself, she's not going to know what to do with it." Maybe it would work. He hadn't exactly been having a great run of luck with girls on his own. Maybe with the Walsh philosophy of love, he could actually get somewhere?

"Xbox?" Easy picked up a control and nodded toward his television.

"No, thanks, I got shit to do." Brandon stood up. "But . . . uh, thanks. This was really helpful." He realized he wanted to e-mail Elizabeth—nothing fancy, just a little note to let her know he got what she was saying, and that it was cool with him. Why the hell not? He was Mr. Open-minded.

OwlNet

SageFrancis: Weird, huh, that Tinsley wasn't at this meeting either? Guess she didn't know there'd be booze.

AlisonQuentin: I def had too much. Would have been good to share!

SageFrancis: Can't believe we've got another partay tomorrow.

AlisonQuentin: Seriously. HTF did Tinsley manage that??

SageFrancis: Think she gave Marymount a little something in return?

AlisonQuentin: Ew! Don't make me barf!

 **Owl**Net

JennyHumphrey: How was the meeting? Sorry I missed it—got distracted at the art studio.

BrettMesserschmidt: Well, Heath's vodka didn't hurt. . . .

JennyHumphrey: The Cinephiles party sounds cool, right?

BrettMesserschmidt: Sure, 'cept for the fact that Cruella de Vil is running the show. Who seems to be MIA tonight.

JennyHumphrey: Maybe she's found some poor schlub to hook up with. Poor guy!

BrettMesserschmidt: 'Kay. I'm going to go see if Kara needs help cleaning up now.

JennyHumphrey: Have FUN!

29

AN EAGER OWL IS WILLING TO TAKE MATTERS INTO HER OWN HANDS.

Of all the things Tinsley Carmichael had done at Waverly—many involving alcohol, some involving drugs, almost all involving boys—she had not once sneaked into a boy's dorm room—or, at least, not alone. And certainly not a *freshman's* dorm room, not even *as* a freshman. But desperate times called for desperate measures. Around nine o'clock, just as the carpet-munching meeting was winding down, Tinsley slipped into a pair of dark Citizens jeans and pulled on her thick black Patagonia fleece over her tissue-thin white T-shirt, zipping it up all the way so that she could sort of disappear in the dark, *her* cloak of invisibility. As she dropped out her window, her rarely used vegan hiking boots (a Christmas gift from her vegetarian father) sinking softly into the mulchy dirt, she felt a thrill of excitement. All right, so she didn't exactly need to sneak out her window, since it wasn't curfew yet . . . but it made things so much more exciting if she felt like she was being devious.

Wolcott, the freshman boys' dorm, was on the far side of Richardson, and Tinsley felt doubly amused at herself for not only sneaking into a boys' dorm room, but for choosing a *freshman* over all the other able-bodied upperclassmen who would certainly be more than willing to open their windows for her. Which is kind of why she was even more excited by the fact that she was sneaking over to see Julian when, for whatever reason, he hadn't come to her the past two times—she felt like he kind of, well, understood her. Knew that she got bored easily, and was presenting her with a challenge.

She stood outside his window and tried to peek in, unable to peer over the windowsill. A light was on and the shade was half pulled down. Tinsley broke a thin branch off a nearby tree and stood on her tiptoes, tapping it gently against the glass. A face appeared and the window flew open—but it wasn't Julian.

Instead, it was some greasy-haired punk kid who was clearly trying to look more grown up than he was by letting a beard grow in. Unfortunately, his face wasn't really up for the challenge, and his growth was patchy at best. His jaw dropped at the sight of her. "What the?" Then his eyes lit up. "Hey? Are you—heyyyyyyyyy!"

He was abruptly cut off as Julian shoved him aside and looked out the window. He looked flustered, to say the least. "Hey. What's up? What're you . . . doing here?"

Not exactly the reaction she'd expected. Tinsley straightened, feeling a little insulted. Maybe he should bring back his roommate—dork that he was, at least he was psyched to see her. Tinsley took a step backward. "I thought I'd drop by," she responded icily. "But if you're busy, don't worry about it. I'll see you some other time."

A smile broke across Julian's face. "I didn't mean it like that." He glanced over his shoulder then leaned forward. "Look, go down to the corner window, okay? Some kid on the floor left this week, and the room's empty. I'll meet you there in, like, twenty seconds, okay?"

Tinsley smiled weakly. "'Kay." He was definitely going to have to do some kissing and making up after that reception. But she couldn't help feeling excited as she stealthily walked along the wall and counted down four windows. Almost immediately, the window opened, and Julian stretched out his hand to help pull her in.

"Thanks." She dusted off her jeans as she surveyed the dark single. It was completely empty except for the dorm room staples that furnished every room: desk, dresser, nightstand, bed. "This kid get kicked out?"

"Nah." Julian shook his head and, to Tinsley's disappointment, pulled out the desk chair and sat down on it. If he wanted to play that way, fine. She scooted onto the desk and let her feet dangle just out of reach of his. Why wasn't he jumping all over her? Was he just teasing her? Since when did freshman boys have those kinds of skills? She was a little confused but also determined not to give in and just ask him what the hell was up. If he was acting like he didn't care, then she might as well too. "It was this kind of weird thing—I guess he had this girlfriend back home, in Montana or something, and you know, they'd like talk for about ten hours every day." Julian leaned his chair back on two legs. "I think he'd even flown home twice this year. But whatever. Eventually he dropped out. Back to Montana, I guess."

"For a girl?" Tinsley asked incredulously, raising her eyebrows. Granted, the kid sounded like kind of a loser. But still—it was sort of a sweet story. She swung her leg out in a wide arc, trying to brush against Julian. But he was just out of a reach. "She must be really hot."

He laughed. "There are other things besides hotness."

Tinsley pretended to be shocked. "Like what?"

"I don't know." Julian yawned and stood up. He seemed anxious, like he couldn't really decide what to do with himself. He wandered over to the closet and opened the door, peering inside at the emptiness. "Like, well, it's nice to have someone you can feel comfortable talking to." He stepped inside, put his hands on the bar, and bent his knees like he was going to do a pull-up. "There's just something very . . . sexy about just talking to a girl."

"Talk is sexy," she agreed. So *that* was what this distance was all about. She was surprised she hadn't thought of it sooner. Julian wanted to talk more. She thought back to the last few times they'd seen each other and realized that it had been pretty physically aggressive—they hadn't been able to keep their hands off each other. Relief flowed through her veins. She knew what the problem was, and how to fix it. Apparently he was the one-in-one-hundred-thousandth guy who'd rather talk than make out. Or at least talk and *then* make out. Well, that was what they were doing now, wasn't it? Tinsley gave a little sigh of happiness and lay down on her back on the desk, staring up out the window at the navy blue night sky. "What else is important to you? In a girl, I mean?"

Julian stepped out of the closet and exhaled thoughtfully, then bent over to retie his shoelace. When he stood up, his cheeks were flushed. "She's got to be able to make me laugh . . . and she can't be afraid to make a fool of herself."

She smiled coyly at him. He was clearly trying to tell her something by saying he was interested in a girl who wasn't afraid to make a fool of herself—like maybe that she needed to throw herself at him for once. She pushed herself off the desk, feeling almost giddy and wondering if maybe it would be a good idea to make their relationship public after all? She walked toward him slowly, enjoying the way he watched her hips as they swung back and forth. *That* was more like it.

Talking and laughing was all well and fine, but there were definitely other parts to a relationship too.

Just as she was about to stretch her arms up and throw them around his neck, a horrible, piercing siren broke through the quiet night air, sending them both jumping apart. Tinsley looked up in disbelief at the flashing red light in the corner of the room—fire alarm. The acrid smell of burnt popcorn suddenly stung her nostrils.

"Shit." Julian tugged her toward the window. "You've got to get out of here—now."

"One kiss before I go." She threw one leg over the windowsill but stopped, waiting. Over the shrill screeching of the fire alarm, she could hear the sounds of loud freshmen boys jostling through the hallway. Any moment they'd be outside, and it would be too late. "Hurry," she hissed.

Julian pressed his lips to hers for a quick kiss, but before he could pull away, she kissed him back passionately, clasping her hand to the back of his neck. After a few seconds, she pulled away, satisfied, and dropped to the ground outside. She dashed away, looking back to see if he was watching her leave.

Unfortunately, he wasn't.

From: BrandonBuchanan@waverly.edu
To: ElizabethJacobs@stlucius.edu
Date: Thursday, October 10, 9:20 P.M.
Subject: It Happened Tomorrow Night?

Elizabeth,

Waverly's film club is having an outdoor screening of *It Happened One Night* tomorrow at 7 P.M. at the Miller farm in Rhinecliff. Don't know if you can get away from campus, but it should be a lot of fun. (Popcorn, old movies, and beer—what more could you ask for?)

About what you were saying today—I get where you're coming from. I just like being with you, and I'm happy to do it on your terms or any terms. Call me Mr. Open!

Hope you can make it tomorrow . . .

Brandon

OwlNet

BrettMesserschmidt: Just e-mailed you the pic. Did you open it yet?

HeathFerro: Hell yeah! It's pretty close up—I can't really tell what body parts are there, though.

BrettMesserschmidt: What, you don't like it??

HeathFerro: R U kidding? I love it! It's the hottest thing I've ever seen—next to the two of you, in the flesh. It's going to bring me sweet dreams tonight.

BrettMesserschmidt: Excellent. You can look forward to many more, as long as you keep your mouth closed.

HeathFerro: I promise, I promise, I promise. Just tell me: is that a belly button?

A WAVERLY OWL NEVER TAKES CRITICISM TO HEART.

"I have a surprise for you today, my little peanuts," Mrs. Silver announced at the beginning of drawing class on Friday afternoon. "You've all been working so hard, so instead of having a regular class today, we're going to have an art show. Hang up what you've been working on—let's say, the favorite three things you've done in the past few weeks—so that we can all see how talented you are." Her eyes twinkled as she picked up a large Tupperware container on her desk. "And everyone, please—take a cupcake!"

"She's always trying to fatten us up," Alison grumbled good-naturedly as she picked up a chocolate cupcake topped with brightly colored sprinkles. She licked a bit of frosting off her thumb. "Just like Hansel and Gretel."

"I don't think you have anything to worry about," Jenny chided. Alison was like a size nothing. She picked up a cupcake with gooey pink frosting and set it down on her desk. "Come on—hang artwork first, eat cupcakes later. Otherwise you'll get frosting on your beautiful drawing of Alan."

Alison giggled. "That's for the figure-drawing class. Do you think we can hang those up now?"

Jenny nodded. "Sure. They're due today, anyway." Jenny thumbed through the stack of drawings on her shelf. Ones from both classes, portraiture and figure drawing, were mixed in with each other. She plucked out one Crayola portrait of Alison she'd done the other day. And then she pulled out two of the drawings that she'd completed last night: one of Julian perched awkwardly in the armchair, pretending to be comfortable, and another one just from his shoulders up, his head thrown back in laughter. It made Jenny smile just to look at them.

"How did you know Alan was my subject?" Alison asked suddenly, unrolling a sheet of thin newsprint paper.

"Lucky guess." Jenny gave her a little hip-check before walking over to the white, smudged walls, filled with hundreds of thumbtack holes from previous art class presentations. She tried not to glance at Easy's shelf, with his sloppily written label, or wonder who *he* had chosen as his subject for the advanced figure-drawing assignment.

After the girls had thumbtacked their drawings to the wall, they stood back to admire them. Alison's was a dreamy-looking charcoal drawing of Alan lying on his side, smiling a sweet, stoned smile. "That's really good." Jenny tilted her head objectively. "He looks so sweet."

"He *is* so sweet," Alison cooed under her breath. "I love yours too. Julian just looks so . . . happy."

After reclaiming their cupcakes the girls wandered around the room, examining the portraits intently. They stepped up close to peer at the brushstrokes or lines, then stepped back to absorb the full effect. Jenny felt like one of those old ladies who travel to art museums in pairs and always have something to say about Monet or Hopper. As the sugar from her cupcake raced through her veins, and she and Alison congratulated their classmates on their portraits, Jenny felt relaxed and happy. Mrs. Silver had put on some kind of Motown music and she was feeling a little swing return to her step.

And she kept smiling to herself thinking about how just last night, she and Julian had been alone in here, flirting and laughing. It gave the whole art building a kind of charge, like she knew something about it that no one else knew. Just thinking about Julian made Jenny feel better about everything. She wondered what this past week would have felt like if she hadn't had him as a distraction. He'd definitely managed to help take her mind off Easy, off Callie, off everything except how nice it was to be at Waverly and to be an artist and to be alive.

"Wow," Alison said under her breath. "Look at this."

Jenny didn't have to glance at the sloppy signature in the corner to tell that the next painting, propped up on an easel, the oil paint still slick and glistening, belonged to Easy. It was hard to say what it was, exactly. It was abstract, and certainly not like any of the other paintings or drawings in the room. Jenny felt a little stab of pride for him—Easy was *such* a good artist. The painting was a hard-to-define system of swirls and thick brushstrokes, of pinks and peaches and pale green highlights, but somehow it pulled together to actually kind of feel like a portrait, of someone or something.

"He's crazy talented," Jenny agreed. Just then, a familiar looking-shape off to the right side of the painting caught her eye, and, like one of the museum ladies, she squinted her eyes and stepped closer. It was a strawberry-shaped mark and it made Jenny think of something, but the more she concentrated, the more that something slipped away from her. She tried to shake her head clear of the thought. Maybe it just reminded her of a strawberry.

"Jenny? Come over here a second, please" She turned at the sound of Mrs. Silver's voice and saw that she was standing in front of her drawings of Julian. She hurried over, and Mrs. Silver placed a doughy hand on her shoulder. "I'd just like to congratulate you, darling. The way you've posed your model emphasizes his extreme height, and the way you've chosen this sort of moment to represent—something as ephemeral and difficult to capture as laughter—well, you do it quite extraordinarily."

"Really?" Jenny's cheeks flushed pink with pride, thrilled to have her work complimented by Mrs. Silver, who, although always encouraging, was never insincere with her praise. She only said things she really meant.

"Oh, yes, dear." Mrs. Silver squeezed her shoulder gently. "And this drawing truly captures the rapport you have with your subject." She patted her frazzled gray hair absentmindedly, reaching for a pencil behind her ear that wasn't there. She focused her gray-blue eyes on Jenny. "It also reveals that you're very fond of him. It's absolutely wonderful that you can translate that emotion into art." Mrs. Silver talked to her a few minutes longer, giving her a formal critique of her lines and contrasts and perspectives. Jenny jotted notes down in her sketch pad but her brain was still fuzzy.

Her portrait of Julian revealed how fond she was of him? Really? Well, wasn't *that* interesting. She had always thought art was the window to her soul. Maybe it was. . . .

To: Undisclosed recipients
From: HeathFerro@waverly.edu
Date: Friday, October 11, 1:45 p.m.
Subject: Pimpin' your rides

Fellow partyphiles,

I've taken the liberty of organizing a shuttle service from the front gate to the Miller farm on behalf of our gracious hostess, the ever-charming and sexilicious Tinsley, who so kindly put together this event. Complimentary beverages included.

Cars are as follows:

Mine—Kara/Brett/me

Next—Callie/Benny/Jenny/Sage

Next—Easy/Alan/Allison/Brandon

All other unlucky fuckers are on your own. Hey, Tinsley, who do you want in your car? I got an extra-special pimpmobile for you and your intimates as thanks for getting the party started.

YEE-freakin'-HAW,

H.F.

OwlNet   Instant Message Inbox

TinsleyCarmichael: Guess who's the lucky boy who gets to ride with me in the waterbed pimpmobile Heath hooked up?

JulianMcCafferty: They have cars with waterbeds in them?

TinsleyCarmichael: Hello? Aren't you psyched? Every boy at Waverly is going to be drooling over how insanely lucky you are to be going with me. Be prepared to sign autographs!

JulianMcCafferty: Can't wait to see the movie.

TinsleyCarmichael: Sweetheart, I guarantee you will not be watching the movie. You'll be living one! Meet me downstairs in an hour.

JulianMcCafferty: Okay.

31

A WAVERLY OWL KEEPS HER DRUNK MOUTH SHUT.

"Whoa!" Jenny squealed as the car turned a corner and Callie slid down the leather seat, careening into her. Callie put her palms up in an effort to stop herself but ended up inadvertently groping Jenny's chest and making her drop her vodka-filled shot glass. Jenny's face flushed—she was glad she and Callie were getting closer, but, um, that was a little much.

"Sorry, Jenny." Callie scrambled off her, tugging her plaid wool Nanette Lepore miniskirt back into place. She huddled her black-nylon-clad knees together—she'd insisted on wearing a skirt even though Jenny had pointed out that she'd be cold, and, even in the warm backseat of the limo, Jenny saw she was shivering. "Didn't mean to feel you up."

"That's okay." Jenny dabbed at the vodka that had spilled on her dark-wash Paige jeans. She was actually kind of glad she wouldn't have to do another shot—it would have been the third round since they left Waverly. "They're kind of hard to avoid." She glanced down at her boobs, which actually looked pretty inoffensive under the kelly green cable-knit cashmere-blend hoodie that had unexpectedly arrived in the mail today from her father, with a note telling her to enjoy those changing autumn leaves.

"Pass the bottle, sweet cheeks!" Benny Cunningham tapped the toe of one of her gold Sigerson Morrison ankle boots against Callie's calf. Callie quickly poured the vodka into her shot glass, sloshing some down the side, before passing the bottle to Benny. Jenny glanced down at those gold boots, thinking they must have cost more than her entire outfit. She briefly wondered if they really were made of gold.

Doing shots on the limo ride from the front gate to the Miller farm had been Callie's idea. "It's a short ride—we need to maximize!" she had cried. Her full bottle of Ketel One only had a few fingers left in the bottom, and the three of them and Sage Francis were already feeling the effects.

"Chicas, I think we're here!" Sage trilled, downing the last of the clear liquor in the bottle. Her corn-silk blond hair was pulled back into a sleek ponytail that bobbed as she pushed open the door to the limo and the four girls tumbled out onto the packed-dirt driveway. Jenny stretched her limbs—the limos were definitely luxurious, but kind of small.

She inhaled a deep breath of fresh air, which smelled like burning leaves and pumpkin pie. The sun had just set, and clusters of kids in thick sweaters were gathered around what had to be the kegs or spreading plaid blankets out on the stiff, yellowing grass. Jenny patted her hair—she'd woven a few loose braids into her long curls.

She stepped away from the car cautiously, trying to judge how drunk she was from the way her boots responded to the ground beneath them. The boots had come with the sweater and were a gift from Vanessa, her brother's girlfriend who was now living in Jenny's old room while she went to NYU. The note said they came from the army-navy surplus store in Dumbo and they looked it—they were deep olive leather lace-ups, plastered with various military-looking badges. Totally funky and unique, exactly the kind of thing Vanessa would think Jenny needed at boarding school to "keep her from getting too J.Crew'd." The best things about them had to be the sturdy, four-inch platform bottoms. Wearing them, Jenny felt almost tall. Or at least not so shrimpy.

Benny poked her in the back. "The beer has to be over there." She pointed toward the crowd gathered off to the side of the picturesque red barn. But Jenny had decided that she was a wee bit tipsy, and so she trailed a little behind the other girls, taking in the scene. The barn stood in front of a large clearing, and the black-and-white film was already flickering across its weathered wall. It was a pretty cool effect—Jenny had never been to a drive-in before, but she imagined this was even better. She spotted Alan St. Girard and Alison lounging on one of the dozen bales of hay that were scattered around on the grass. Alison had her legs stretched across his lap, and he was sticking a piece of hay behind her ear. Unexpectedly, Jenny felt a pang of envy—*she* wanted to have someone looking at her like that and tickling her with hay.

Her eyes scanned all the tall figures in the crowd, surprising herself that she wasn't looking for Easy, but Julian.

"Say something for the camera, ladies!" Ryan Reynolds popped up out of nowhere, a sleek silver digital camcorder the size of a wallet glued to his face.

Sage pursed her highly glossed lips and struck a pose for the video camera. "Priorities, dummy." Benny grabbed Sage by the wrist and tugged her toward the barn, where the keg crowd was growing larger. "Beer first, flirting later." Ryan disappeared into the crowd, disappointed. Jenny lagged behind the others, feeling uncomfortable. It was nice that Benny and Sage and Callie included her in their little group, and she had been able to feel everyone sort of watching them the moment they got out of the car, like they were something special. Like she was something special. And that was kind of nice—but at the same time, where was Brett? She needed someone real to talk to.

Another sleek black car pulled up the dirt driveway, sending up giant clouds of dust. Jenny watched with relief as Kara and Brett and Heath piled out, giggling like schoolgirls. Heath had on the blond wig from the other night, and he threw his arms around both girls' shoulders and whispered something in Brett's ear that made her toss back her red hair and shriek with laughter.

"All right, who else thinks it's totally bizarre that Heath and Brett are hooking up?" Benny demanded, unbuttoning her black velvet riding blazer. "I thought she *loathed* him."

Jenny saw Callie roll her eyes and stumble slightly on the uneven ground before quickly righting herself and acting like nothing had happened. "Um . . . I don't think it's *Heath* she's hooking up with, if you know what I mean."

Benny and Sage exchanged glances, but Jenny had to quickly turn away. Wait a second. Did Callie really know about Brett and Kara, too? *How?* And why was she babbling to Benny and Sage about it? Well, maybe they hadn't understood her. Or maybe they'd chalk it up to the ramblings of a drunk girl.

But from the look on Benny's face, she *definitely* knew what Callie meant.

OwlNet   Email Inbox

To: BrandonBuchanen@waverly.edu
From: ElizabethJacobs@stluciusacademy.edu
Date: Friday, October 11, 7:09 P.M.
Subject: Late

B,

Running late and still have to jump in the shower. (Get that smile off your face. . . .) I'll meet you at the farm, okay?

Luv,

El

OwlNet   Instant Message Inbox

EasyWalsh: R U here yet?

CallieVernon: Yup. Just pulled up with the girls. Movie's on, where R U?

EasyWalsh: Inside the barn, waiting for you to sneak away.

CallieVernon: Oh, yeah? Well, as soon as I get a chance.

EasyWalsh: Hurry, darlin'. . . .

32

WAVERLY OWLS ONLY PLAY HARD-TO-GET UNTIL THEY'RE GOTTEN.

Callie started to stand in line with Benny and Sage for beer, but she kept getting jostled, and everyone seemed to be stepping on her toes (which were already uncomfortable, crammed into her half-size-too-small patent leather Taryn Rose wedges). And after the text from Easy, her mind was elsewhere—she knew she probably shouldn't be alone with him after she'd been drinking, but the truth was, *whenever* she was with him, she had to fight the urge to throw herself at him. It was like there was something inside her that responded to his frequency or something.

Still, she wasn't ready to come running the second he called. He could certainly wait for her. She had to enjoy the party for a while, didn't she? Callie rubbed her hands up and down her arms, trying to warm herself up. She looked up at the gorgeous, navy blue night sky. The few stars that were starting to peek out looked like ice chips. She patted the tiny bulge in the hip pocket of her miniskirt. Before leaving her dorm room, she'd pulled open the drawer of her nightstand in search of a hair clip, and had been confronted by the giant box of condoms that had been sitting there since the start of school. She'd bought it out of wishful thinking, hoping that sex would save her and Easy's relationship. But it hadn't worked out that way—it was only by breaking up that they'd been able to save it. Tonight, though, she had put one in her pocket. Better safe than sorry.

Two seconds after deciding to let Easy sweat it out, the eighth person stepped on Callie's toes, and she decided maybe it would be a little warmer—and less crowded, certainly—inside the barn. She slowly extricated herself from the beer line and walked around the corner of the barn, pretending to be searching her red leather tiny Hobo International bag for her cigarettes. The sounds of the movie and the crowd became fainter as she made her way toward the barn door, using the light from her cell phone to make sure she didn't step in any cow shit or on any other disgusting barn-bred things. She peeked inside the half-closed door and saw a faint light at the back of the barn, some scary-looking shadows projected on the huge walls. She shivered a little, only partly from the cold. Could barns be haunted like old houses? And was Easy really in here, or was she all alone?

"Easy?" she whispered loudly, her voice wavering in the darkness.

"Hey!" At the sound of his voice, Callie's heart sped up, and when his head popped up over the side of the last stall, she had to catch her breath. She hadn't realized how anxious she was to see him until she'd kind of thought he wasn't there. "Over here." The faint light disappeared and then reappeared as Easy stepped out of the stall and stood at the end of the barn, holding a flashlight.

Callie walked slowly toward him, her knees wobbling a little as she stepped over the uneven barn floor, half covered with hay. She didn't know why she was so nervous. Maybe because she didn't want him to know she was drunk already. Maybe because she could feel his dark blue eyes watching her every step. She couldn't help but feel completely beautiful under his appreciative eyes—skinny legs, too-short skirt, bulky turtleneck sweater and all. Her cheeks flushed with pleasure as she stopped two feet in front of him. "You're missing the party," she chided, only because it was the first thing that came to her mind.

Easy smiled at her. "I've seen movies before. And drunks," he added playfully.

Callie stared at his cheekbones, which, in the glowing light of the lantern, looked even more striking and defined. He wore a paint-splattered flannel shirt that she was dying to rub her face against, with his beat-up tan cords that had a hole forming in the knee and a splotch of blue paint on the right thigh. He stood the flashlight on its end on the floor of the old horse stall, which didn't smell as horsey as the stables, so thankfully it must not be used anymore. Callie noticed for the first time that Easy had sort of cozied up the stall. A thick, nest-like bed of hay had been formed, and a heavy Scottish wool blanket covered the whole thing. A maroon fleece Waverly blanket was balled up in a corner, presumably to lie down *under,* and a tattered copy of *The Great Gatsby* was lying facedown on the blanket.

"Were you *reading?*" Callie teased, trying to hide the fact that she was really moved by the way Easy had set up this space for her—for *them.* She shivered again, even though it was warmer inside than out. She couldn't even hear the movie anymore.

"Nah." Easy scratched his head, embarrassed. "I was just waiting for you."

Callie felt her resolve weaken, but not completely disappear. She crossed her arms across her chest and tried not to look straight at him, sort of like trying not to look straight at the sun. It was too painful. But then she noticed the three red roses, lying at the other corner of the blanket, as if waiting for her. "Why three?" she asked, a lump in her throat.

Easy coughed. "I don't know. A dozen seemed . . . too corny." He ran his hand through his unruly curls. "And one just seemed like not enough." His eyes were lowered, and he peered up at Callie through his thick, dark eyelashes. She pictured him, standing in the stuffy little Rhinecliff florist's shop, debating as to how many roses would be "enough." That was so un-Easy-like.

She melted. *Easy.* Before he could do anything else, she threw her arms around his neck and kissed him. His mouth met hers eagerly and she wrapped her fingers around the curls at the nape of his neck.

"Let's lie down," she murmured after a few intense minutes of kissing. They fell onto the wool blanket and Callie snuggled up against Easy's long, lean body, wishing she weren't wearing her bulky turtleneck. She just couldn't get close enough to him—she wanted their skin to touch.

As if reading her mind, Easy toyed with the bottom of her sweater. "Can this come off?" In response, Callie sat up and kissed his neck, then slowly tugged the sweater up and over her shoulders, revealing her sheer pink Chantelle demi-bra with a tiny black tulip in the center.

She felt his breath against her skin. "Pretty," he whispered, running his lips over her shoulders. His fingers trembled as they traced her collarbone.

"Hey, did your teacher like your painting?" she asked suddenly, sitting up to look at him. She started thinking of the last time she and Easy had kissed. It felt like so long ago when he had told her he loved her. He loved her. Easy Walsh loved Callie Vernon. Her flesh instantly goose-bumped, which she really hoped wasn't a total turnoff. She wanted him to say it again. Things felt different now—right again, or even *more* right than before they'd broken up.

This was the way it was supposed to be, she thought, for your first time.

"What? Oh." Easy rubbed his hand along her left arm. "Are you cold?" He grabbed the fleece blanket and threw it over them.

Callie shook off his hand impatiently. "She didn't like it?"

The sides of his mouth curled up into his familiar crooked grin. "She loved it. She wanted to know where I found such a beautiful model."

"Liar!" Callie put her hands on Easy's shoulders and pushed

him down to the blanket. "*Your* turn." She pulled at the buttons on his flannel shirt impatiently. While just a few minutes ago she'd been thinking about running her face against it, now that wasn't good enough—she wanted to touch his skin, to feel the warmth of his body against hers. He helped her push the buttons through the holes, feeling her urgency.

"Hey." Easy stopped with his shirt and grabbed Callie's chin gently, staring straight into her eyes. "What are we, uh, doing?"

"Don't make me spell it out." She reached into her hip pocket and pulled out the shiny turquoise-and-silver package, slipping it into his hand in one smooth move.

Easy stroked her hair. "Really? You're ready and everything?" She thought she'd never seen him look so happy before.

She pulled his shirt off his shoulders and pressed her ear to his chest, where she could hear his heart almost thudding through his skin. She'd never been more ready for anything in her life.

A WAVERLY OWL CAN ONLY TRY SO HARD TO BE SOMETHING HE'S NOT.

Brandon stood off to the side of the barn, sipping his beer and scanning the crowd for Elizabeth's familiar blond head. No luck. He'd gotten her e-mail that she'd be late, but the movie was half over. Not that he was following it—no one was, really. Kids were lying on blankets, smoking cigarettes and drinking Heath's crappy keg beer, huddled together ostensibly for warmth. The sight of all the cuddling couples made him miss Elizabeth even more. Who the hell wanted to watch goony Alan St. Girard, who could never be bothered to shave his nasty beard scruff, sucking face with sweet little Alison Quentin?

And then he saw her, standing over by the kegs, wearing the pleather motorcycle jacket she'd had on when he first saw her, a red pashmina wrapped around her neck. Brandon breathed a huge sigh of relief and took the first step over to her.

Except just as he did that, she leaned forward and touched the arm of the guy she was talking to. He could tell from the way her red-gloved hand flexed that she was giving him a squeeze. The same way she had once squeezed *his* arm.

And now she was doing it to Brian fucking Atherton.

Brandon counted to twelve, as his father had always insisted on doing when angry, because "after twelve seconds, big things don't seem so big." Twelve seconds of watching Elizabeth lean closer and closer to that asswipe, tossing her head back with laughter, the white curve of her neck almost glittering in the moonlight. And all for Atherton, who was staring at her as if she were a Big Mac and he had the munchies. Brandon stormed over to them, not noticing whose blankets he stepped on. "Down in front," someone called out. People giggled.

Suddenly, he stopped. What was he going to do, punch the guy out? He wasn't about to make a fool of himself in front of a dickweed like Atherton. He tried to remember what Easy had said to him. Give her space, and she'll come to you. Brandon clenched his fists. He'd told her he'd give her space. He knew it wasn't fair of him to change his mind twenty-four hours later.

He stalked over to the pair, still trembling with anger but determined not to show it. Elizabeth smiled when she saw him and waved a red-gloved hand at him. She looked so happy to see him. "Hey, babe!" She leaned toward him and planted a kiss on his cheek, leaving behind the smell of patchouli.

"Hey, man, what's up?" Atherton held up his palm for a high five, a shit-eating grin plastered to his face that seemed to say, "You think this is your *girlfriend*?"

Brandon ignored the high five and nodded toward the film projector. "I heard some freshman girls talking about you back there."

"No shit." Atherton's eyes scanned the crowd. "Were they hot?"

"Yeah," Brandon said sheepishly. "Back by the projector."

"Cool." Atherton made a gun with his fingers and made a clicking noise with his mouth to pull the trigger. He leered at Elizabeth. "I'll catch you cats later."

Elizabeth didn't even watch him leave. Instead, she put her gloved hand on Brandon's forearm and squeezed. Her other hand held a half-empty beer. "Good to see you, sexy."

Brandon could barely stand it. Did it really not matter to her that thirty seconds ago she'd been squeezing some other guy's arm exactly like this? "Yeah, uh, you too. You look like you're, uh, having a good time." He tried to keep his tone light, but he couldn't keep the bitterness from seeping in.

Elizabeth looked up at him in surprise, her cheeks rosy from the cold. "What does that mean?"

Brandon rubbed his hand over his eyes, trying to make himself keep quiet. He couldn't. "Atherton! He's such a sleaze."

Elizabeth stiffened and quickly withdrew her hand from his arm. She crossed her arms in front of her chest. "Wait a second—are you mad at me? I was going to come and find you as soon as I finished my beer. What happened to Mr. Open?"

"I know," Brandon admitted, kicking the ground with the toe of his polished John Varvatos boot. "But I didn't think that would mean having to actually *watch* you flirt with other guys."

"So what *does* this mean, then?" Her eyebrows furrowed together in frustration, and Brandon could tell she was actually really surprised—and hurt—that he was acting this way. But there was really no other way he could act. As soon as Atherton had disappeared, so had all his bravado. That wasn't what he wanted—to see the girl he was crazy about drooling all over someone else, and not be bothered by it? That was fucked up.

Brandon stuffed his cold palms into the pockets of his Rock & Republic jeans. "I guess it means Mr. Open is closed." And he turned and walked away.

WATCH OUT! WAVERLY OWLS CAN BE A CARNIVOROUS SPECIES.

Brett leaned back, enjoying the feel of Kara's fingers playing with her hair. Kara was sitting cross-legged on the thick cotton quilt Brett had brought to spread out, and Brett's head was lying on a bunched up sweatshirt on her lap. Normally she would have been worried about how that looked, but she'd had a few beers by now and she didn't care so much. Besides, Brett's own hands were playing with Heath's hair, who was lying contentedly on his side, his head resting against Brett's flat stomach. There was something very soothing about the whole thing—of course it was totally weird how suddenly Heath was their good friend, but Brett had started to genuinely like him. He seemed totally sincere about keeping their secret, and it was kind of fun for the girls to pal around with him, leaving everyone else wondering what the hell was going on. It was a pretty convenient smoke screen, she had to admit.

Not that she liked feeling like she and Kara were fooling everyone. That wasn't it. But it was important to keep their secret, well, secret. Things between them were so new still—Brett was trying to follow Jenny's advice to just "go with it" and not overanalyze everything. She couldn't do that if the whole world, or the whole Waverly population at least, was whispering about her.

Heath's pocket vibrated and he pulled out his phone to read a text. "Ladies, I hate to leave you, but someone's smoking something, and I need to be part of it." He clearly had a hard time pulling his eyes away from them as he stood up. "Don't do anything good without me. Or if you do, take pictures." He kept his voice low so people around them couldn't hear.

"Do you want me to get us some more beer?" Brett sat up and turned toward Kara once Heath had cantered off toward the cornfields.

The film flickered and cut to a day scene, lighting up Kara's face. Brett could read from her expressive greenish-brown eyes that she was wondering if Brett was trying to avoid being alone with her in public. But all she said was, "Sure."

Under cover of the crumpled sweatshirt, Brett put her hand on Kara's knee and squeezed gently. In a perfect world, she'd be able to lean in and kiss her right now, tasting her grapefruit lip gloss. Brett felt a deep ache in her stomach but ignored it and got to her feet. She looked down at Kara in her black turtleneck sweater and gray down vest from her mother's athletic line of clothing. It was so weird to be looking at a girl and thinking about how badly she wanted to kiss her. "Be right back," she promised.

Brett wove her way through the crowds of people sprawled out on blankets. The crowd watching the movie had thinned out a little, which was not surprising, as there seemed to be a multitude of other outlets for entertainment offered by the unsupervised, off-campus evening. How the hell had Tinsley managed to get this approved? And where *was* Tinsley, anyway? But Brett's musings faded to the back of her mind as she noticed that people were sort of hushing one another as she approached. Were people . . . *talking* about her? Her face flushed immediately, but she managed to make her way over to the keg line gracefully enough.

However, as she tapped the toe of her Stuart Weitzman clog against the hard, grassy ground, she heard something in front of her in line that almost turned her blood instantly into ice. "Brett? You mean she's . . . *gay?*"

She felt sick. Heath fucking Ferro. Of course. That lowlife, degenerate hornbag *squealer*. Immediately, Brett spun on her heel and dashed back toward her blanket, obviously forgetting all about the beer, and stepping on several other blankets carelessly. Out of nowhere, a very drunk and staggering Ryan Reynolds popped up and slung his arm around her lean shoulders "Think I can join in sometime?"

"Fuck off," she hissed, shrugging off his arm and continuing her stomp across the lawn, blinded slightly by the darkness and her anger. Finally, she was able to sink down on the blanket where Kara was sitting.

"What's the matter?" Kara asked, immediately knowing something was wrong.

"Where's Heath?" Brett could barely get the words out, her whole body was shaking so much. "I'm going to kill him, right now. In front of the entire world."

Kara's eyes widened. "What are you *talking* about?"

Brett pressed her lips together, trying to calm down. But her heart was beating a thousand times a minute and all she could think about was punching Heath right in his stupid, cocky face. "He told everyone. They all know. Everyone knows."

"Ohhhhh." Kara glanced around her, and Brett knew she wanted to hug her or grab her hand or do something to make it feel better, and it made her feel even more pissed off by the whole situation. "But he wouldn't do that."

"Well, he did." Brett ran a hand through her bobbed red hair, forgetting all about how nice it had felt to have Kara combing it with her fingers ten minutes ago. But everything had changed now—everything. All because fuckface Heath couldn't keep his goddamned mouth shut. He had to gloat, didn't he? Share it with the whole world? "Who else could have told?"

Kara bit her lip, worriedly. "I don't know. Maybe it's not the end of the world if people find out?" A lock of her silky hair fell in front of her face, partly hiding her questioning eyes.

Brett looked at Kara's sweet, pretty face, wishing she could agree. She knew it was silly to be embarrassed about being with Kara—but having people stare at her like she was a circus freak was the last thing she wanted. She'd just gotten over people finding out about her totally tacky family, and frankly, she didn't like being at the center of the Waverly gossip tornado. Unfortunately, it seemed she was in the eye of the storm.

A WAVERLY OWL KNOWS HOW TO EXTRACT HERSELF
FROM AN UNCOMFORTABLE SITUATION.

"But we're going to play I Never. You can't go!" Verena Arneval protested as Jenny stood up and stretched her legs. Jenny hadn't quite felt like herself all night, but she wasn't really sure why not. Brett and Kara and Heath seemed to be in their own little world that she didn't really want to interrupt. Callie had disappeared about an hour ago, leaving her to drink with Verena and Alison and Alan and a bunch of others. It was fun, but . . . it wasn't really that fun. Jenny's brain was feeling slow from beer, and if she drank any more, she would be drunk.

Not to mention the disaster that had happened the last time everyone played I Never. No, thank you. She shook her head resolutely, stepping away from the bales of hay she'd been sitting on. Jenny played with the hood of her green sweater and glanced up at the black-and-white film still playing on the side of the barn. She hadn't exactly been paying attention, but something about it seemed so . . . romantic. "I'm just going to walk around a little. I'll be back." She heard Ryan's camera click as he took a photograph of her ass as she walked away. Sigh.

Jenny had never actually seen the inside of a real barn before, only in the movies and on TV, so she meandered toward the building, stepping around groups of people making out on blankets or playing games involving slamming down as much of the now-warm beer as possible. Snippets of conversations about Brett and Kara and their illicit love affair hit Jenny's ears more than once. *Yikes.* Looked like the secret was already full-fledged gossip. She squinted her eyes but couldn't see Brett's fire-engine-red hair anywhere. She was such a private person, it was going to kill her to have her secrets made so public.

Jenny also scanned the crowd for signs of another familiar body but didn't see him. Maybe that was why she was feeling so depressed tonight.

Her boots kicked their way through the grass as she turned the corner to the other side of the barn, and there was blessed silence. The sounds of the movie disappeared. Jenny leaned against the weathered wood of the barn and stared up at the fat, silvery moon hanging like a globe in the navy night sky, wisps of clouds half-covering it.

She peeked her head inside the barn door, surprised to see two tiny flecks of red light at the far end of the barn. Curious, she squinted again, not quite sure what she was looking at. As her vision cleared, two things happened at the exact same instant: the clouds moved to let some moonlight shine fully in the barn, illuminating the interior, and one of the red flecks moved. It was Callie, standing up in the last stall, a cigarette in her hand, and her perfect, bare shoulders glowing in the moonlight. The stall wall hid the rest of her body, but it wasn't hard to guess from her naked shoulders that she probably wasn't wearing a strapless dress.

Especially when Jenny noted that the other fleck of red belonged to someone else's cigarette—Easy's.

Her hands started to shake and tears instinctively sprang to her eyes as she realized something she probably should have known all along: they were together again. And then, in a flash of insight, she saw the abstract portrait Easy had hung up in art class today. That strawberry shape that had seemed so familiar to Jenny—it was the birthmark on Callie's lower back, something only someone who had seen her recently in a bikini, or a bra, or nothing at all—would have been able to portray so perfectly. She felt her lower lip start to tremble. They were together again, but that wasn't the worst part. Callie had lied to her. She'd thought they were really friends, but she'd been so . . . wrong.

Jenny spun around and walked away from the barn quickly, away from the party. She wasn't sure exactly where she was going, but she knew she had to get away. She was tired of drinking beer and playing stupid games and having people she thought were her friends lie to her. As she plowed ahead, a horrible image of Easy and Callie came to mind, of the two of them, laughing—at her, for believing they were all friends. She could almost hear Callie saying, "I can't believe she really thought you liked her better than me." Jenny stumbled over something on the ground—a corncob. She kicked it hard with her boot, sending it flying through the air and thwacking into some kind of metal silo in front of her with a satisfying thud.

"You'd better watch where you're aiming that. You might hit an innocent bystander." Jenny looked up, and her heart almost stopped in her throat. *Julian.* He was sitting on some sort of tree stump off to the side of the silo, an empty plastic beer cup in his hands.

An amazing feeling flooded through her entire body—that wonderful, unexpected feeling that comes when, totally out of the blue, you're given something that you hadn't even realized you wanted or needed or craved. Like that morning, when Jenny had opened the package from her father and pulled out a Tupperware container of pumpkin-chocolate-chip muffins from the bakery on Amsterdam Avenue that were quite possibly the most delicious and comforting things on the planet.

But that obviously didn't compare to the way she felt when Julian appeared before her, all by himself, just when she thought things were at their absolute worst. He was the one she'd been looking for all night.

"What are you doing out here?" Jenny asked, suddenly flustered that things were happening so fast. She'd just come from seeing her ex-boyfriend, the boyfriend she thought maybe she loved, naked with his ex-girlfriend, her roommate who had made a pact with her that they were done with Easy for good. So much for pacts. She shivered to shake off the awful feeling that she'd been majorly duped in some massive con. "In the dark?"

As usual, he had a ready answer. "I gave myself a time-out."

Jenny laughed. "So you mean you're hiding?" For some reason, she always felt the urge to be bold around Julian—it was like that part of her brain that naturally prevented her mouth from actually saying the first thing that came to her mind somehow shut off around him. But at the same time, she got the feeling that he didn't mind.

"Well . . ." Julian drew out the word. He squeezed the plastic cup in his hands, crumpling it up noisily. Finally, he sighed. "Sort of." Then he patted the stump next to him invitingly. she sank down next to him, knowing better than to ask who he was hiding from.

As they sat together on the bench, Jenny was completely aware of how close her leg was to his. Only about an inch of air separated them. Neither of them said anything for a few moments, listening instead to the faint sounds of the movie in the distance. Weirdly, it wasn't uncomfortable at all.

At last, Julian spoke, his breath visible in the darkness. "This is kind of a cool place. I just wish, you know, it wasn't such a . . . circus." His longish blondish-brown hair was tucked behind his ears, skimming the shoulders of his olive green fleece jacket. Jenny looked down at their feet—his vintage black Tretorns were enormous, especially next to her small, round-toed boots. But somehow, they looked, well, kind of cute together.

"Do you want to go back and watch the movie?" she asked, hoping he'd say no.

He turned his head toward her, the moonlight lighting up his deep brown eyes so that Jenny could practically count the little flecks of gold in them. "No," he answered simply.

Her cheeks flushed, and her hands, inside the pockets of her sweater, started to sweat just a little. What was going on here? Was this . . . was something . . . really happening? Jenny suddenly felt a little nervous. "This, uh, kind of weird thing happened, just before." She felt, for some reason, the need to explain this to him—she wasn't quite sure why, but she felt like it was something she had to do. "I walked into the barn, and Callie and Easy were in there, kind of . . ." She trailed off. It looked like they'd been having sex, but she wasn't going to start spreading rumors. She knew how much that sucked. "Well, you know. Together."

"Oh." If Jenny hadn't been so acutely aware of exactly how close Julian's leg was to hers, she might not have noticed at that moment how he moved himself, almost imperceptibly, about a centimeter away from her. "Wow. That sucks." His eyes turned down to stare at his shoes, and she wondered if he was thinking that hers looked cute next to his. "That must have been really hard for you—to see him with someone else, I mean."

Jenny shook her head slowly, and before she realized what exactly she was doing, she'd put her hand on his arm. "That's not it, really." Julian's fleece was worn out and soft as a baby's blanket beneath her hand. It was kind of exciting to be touching him like that, and he immediately turned his face back toward her, quizzically. "It was weird, but not because of Easy." As if it had a mind of its own, Jenny's thumb started to stroke

Julian's arm and she realized that since she'd been talking to him, she hadn't once thought about how cold she was. "I'm over him, and now I kind of know for sure that we were never really meant to be."

"Yeah?" Julian asked, his eyebrows raised as if he wasn't sure he should believe her. But then he glanced down at her small hand on his jacket and seemed to believe in that. He shifted a little on the stump to face her.

She nodded. "Besides, I kind of like someone else now." She pressed her lips together to keep from smiling. There was that boldness again.

Her heart was beating at a crazy speed, and her fingers were cold, and the bark from the stump was kind of poking into the back of her thigh. And yet . . . she didn't want the moment to end. Especially not when Julian touched her hand with his. He cleared his throat. "I was kind of hoping," he admitted, his voice deep and a little husky.

She felt a curl of dark hair fall into her face, and she pushed it delicately behind one ear. Julian traced a finger along her wrist, something she wouldn't have imagined could feel as good as it did, and turned her face up toward his. She couldn't believe his hand was touching hers, and as he leaned in toward her, she still wasn't convinced it was actually happening.

His full lips paused an inch from hers. "I've been thinking about you all day," he whispered. Then he kissed her, his warm mouth meeting hers. Her last thought before she closed her eyes was that his face, which looked so adorable hanging on the wall of the art studio, was even better close up.

36

A WAVERLY OWL KEEPS HER COOL, EVEN WHEN
SHOCKED AND PISSED AS HELL.

Tinsley flicked open Julian's Zippo, watching the flame
spring up and illuminate the dark night. She had the
lighter, but she wanted the boy. Where the hell was
he? She clicked the lighter closed in frustration. She hadn't
seen him since the ride over, when he'd been acting . . . weird.
Heath had been kind enough to reserve for her the most over-
the-top vehicle the rental agency had in its fleet: a Hummer
with a waterbed in the back. A total shagmobile. But from
the very second she had met Julian outside the front gate,
he'd been acting a little, well, distant. Tinsley had written it
off at the time as playing hard-to-get, an attempt on his part
to get her riled up. But really, she shouldn't have to be working that hard. In her wide-leg navy velvet Armani pants that
hugged her ass like it was their job, and her ecru Anna Sui
lace top that allowed the outline of her chocolate brown La

Perla camisole to be deliciously traceable, she shouldn't have to be working at *all*.

But Julian's distance made her even more attracted to him, and she knew that was what he wanted. He'd snagged Tinsley Carmichael, after all, and he knew he'd have to stay on his toes to keep her. And so, as they'd lain together on the waterbed, she'd massaged his shoulders, getting increasingly turned on the more he resisted her charms. Just as she'd been about to make a real move, the Hummer had pulled up to the barn. She wished she'd thought to tell the driver to take the long way.

After setting up the movie, Tinsley had glanced around and seen that Julian had disappeared. She rubbed her hands up and down her arms, the fabric of her satiny BCBG cropped jacket cold against her skin. She wished the price of looking so good didn't have to be freezing to death. Her eyes had scanned the crowd repeatedly over the next hour or so as she flitted back and forth, flirting with guys she didn't give a shit about and talking to girls who bored her to tears, wondering how hard-to-get Julian was willing to be.

Finally, her anticipation gave way to irritation, and halfway through the movie, she had had enough of the cat-and-mouse game. She abruptly stood up from the picnic table where she'd been watching Parker DuBois, the sexy senior from Belgium, smoke cloves alone by himself on a blanket, actually watching the movie. Tinsley was tempted to go over and sit next to him, but then she realized she was only interested in doing so if it would make Julian jealous—and since he was MIA, that seemed counterproductive.

Instead, she strode around the barn, for a moment excited by the idea that maybe he was waiting for her inside there. Maybe he'd been planning on surprising her this whole time, and she'd been stupidly wasting time they could have been using to get it on. But just as she paused at the dark, partly open barn door, she saw movement in the distance, next to the silo. She recognized Julian, sitting down on something in the dark, and just as she was about to call out his name in triumph—she had found him!—she realized that he was not alone.

And not only was he not alone, his face was glued to someone else's.

Only an idiot would have missed the tender way Julian's hand stroked the girl's arm. It was straight out of a cheesy date movie—leading guy touches leading girl in intimate, affectionate way that leaves the audience no doubt as to his feelings for her. For a moment, Tinsley could do nothing but stare, transfixed. She could practically imagine herself in one of the cozy, reclining chairs of a multiplex, watching this scene, somewhere near the end of a bad romantic comedy. Some corny song would start playing. Cue credits.

Suddenly, she came out of her daze, her anger flaring through her veins like an electric current. What. The. Fuck. Julian, who she'd been fantasizing about all week, thinking about every spare second—and here he was, sucking face with someone else? How dare he!

Tinsley's pulse quickened as Julian pulled back and she could see the girl's face. Her eyes zoomed in like a camera lens.

Jenny.

Something in her snapped. Jenny Humphrey, who thought she could just stride right into Waverly Academy with her puke-yellow suede ballet flats and her tiny upturned nose and her enormous boobs and steal any guy she wanted, regardless of who they happened to be seeing at the moment. She'd stolen Easy from Callie, and now she'd set her hooks into the one boy Tinsley actually cared about. Even in the moonlight, Tinsley could see her flushed pink cheeks with their sprinkles of freckles, her curly hair falling in annoyingly bohemian little braids.

A wail rose up in Tinsley's throat, but she somehow found the composure to keep herself from screaming at the top of her lungs. Instead her fists clenched, and, realizing there was something in her right hand, she glanced down. Julian's lighter.

She flicked it open absentmindedly, still staring at Julian and Jenny, knowing that the image of the two of them kissing was going to remain in her mind for a long, long time. Disgusted, furious, and far more hurt than she'd ever have admitted, Tinsley swung her arm and sent Julian's lighter flying through the night air. She spun around on the heel of her patent leather Miss Sixty ankle-strap pumps, not even looking to see where it landed.

37

A WAVERLY OWL LOOKS TO SEE WHO IS WATCHING

BEFORE THROWING A FIT.

Heath Ferro must die. Heath Ferro must die. Brett could barely think of anything else besides how badly she wanted to strangle him. Of course they never should have trusted him—just when she was starting to feel like he was a real friend, she had to find out that this whole thing was some sort of amusing game to him, one that he couldn't resist bragging about to the entire world.

She caught sight of his familiar dirty blond rumpled head over by the tapped kegs, a thin white joint held to his lips. She stormed over to him, her bobbed hair slipping out of the rhinestone barrettes that held it away from her face. When she got to his side, she edged Alan St. Girard out of the way and pulled the smoking joint from Heath's lips.

"Wha—?" Heath started, but Brett cut him off. She pushed him a few steps away from the others.

"How could you?" she demanded, trying to keep her voice at a whisper. But it was hard when she was so freaking mad. "How could you fucking tell everyone about me and Kara? I can't believe we were stupid enough to trust you!"

"Wait, what are you talking about?" Heath's face immediately broke into a panic. His cheeks were flushed from the beer and weed, but he wasn't even glancing at the joint Brett had stolen. His hazel eyes were wide with confusion and terror. "No way did I tell anyone about you guys! I swear on . . . like, whatever you want!" He ran his hands through his hair as if he was trying to pull it out.

Brett paused. "You didn't say anything? To anyone?"

"No!" It must have been the combination of beer and drugs and frustration, but Brett would have sworn she could see tears starting to form in the corner of Heath's eyes. "What —what about the photos?" he asked, almost timidly.

She put her hand on his arm and gave him a little squeeze. He clearly wasn't the culprit here. But if Heath hadn't spilled, who had? "Okay, I'm sorry. I'm just . . . I don't know." She handed the half-burned joint back to him. "I didn't mean to flip out at you. But who else could have told everyone? The only person I said anything to was . . ." Her voice trailed off.

Jenny.

Brett was suddenly aware of the silence around her. The sound of Clark Gable and Claudette Colbert chattering was the only thing she could hear. With a sinking feeling in the pit of her stomach, she realized that everyone around her could hear perfectly what she was saying to Heath. If anyone hadn't known about her and Kara before, they did now. Brett wished the ground would open under her feet and swallow her whole, and she could disappear from this miserable scene without a trace.

She was about to turn her head and see how many people were actually watching, when Heath pointed at something in the air. "Holy shit. Is that . . . smoke?"

Almost as quickly as the crowd had quieted down, it immediately buzzed to life. "Ohmigod." The acrid smell of burning wood hung in the air, and quickly the party became absolute chaos as everyone scrambled to pick up their things and run away from the barn. Brett stared stupidly at the flames that were starting to flicker into the black night sky. She took a step closer. How the hell had this happened? "Is it on fire?"

Around the corner of the barn, Callie and Easy suddenly appeared, Easy fumbling to button up his shirt, Callie tugging down her thick black sweater. Under her short skirt, her legs were totally bare, and she was carrying one shoe in each hand. Uh, hello? Pieces of hay or straw were sticking out of her hair like she'd been rolling around in it, which, judging from the tender way Easy placed his hand on the small of her back as they raced away, she must have been doing.

"Fire!" Easy shouted at the top of his lungs, as if everyone was too caught up in seeing him and Callie appear out of nowhere, half-dressed, to notice the fact that the enormous red barn behind them was going up in flames.

A WAVERLY OWL KNOWS THAT WHERE THERE'S SMOKE, THERE'S USUALLY A WHOLE LOTTA FIRE.

Callie huddled against Easy in the backseat of an over-crowded limo—no one seemed to care about who rode where now that the fire department was attempting to put out the enormous blaze—still unable to believe every-thing that had just happened. As the Waverly Owls frantically scrambled to their waiting rental cars, eager to speed away from the scene as quickly as possible, Callie had seen Tinsley manage to turn off the projector and scoop up the film equipment. No one seemed to know what had happened to the barn, exactly. The scene reminded her of something from *Gone with the Wind,* where Scarlett O'Hara and everyone else had to flee a burning Atlanta. Creepy.

As Easy stroked her smoke-scented hair, all Callie could think about was what had happened between them. They'd actually . . . had sex. Made love. Whatever. Everything between them was different now—they were somehow connected in this totally intimate, personal, incomparable way. She leaned into his shoulder, not caring how obvious it was that they were together. After all, pretty much everyone had seen them running from the barn half-clothed, and now Callie felt like everyone in the car was staring at her bare legs. Thank God she'd remembered to shave.

She was kind of in a haze after what had happened—the sex part, not the fire. In sort of a twisted, dramatic way, it seemed kind of satisfying that the barn had burned down. It felt like something out of a novel, though Callie couldn't have said *which* novel. But now the place where she and Easy lost their virginity no longer existed—which was far preferable to knowing that some day some dirty cow could be standing in the exact spot where they'd proved their love to each other.

After the car dropped everyone off at the front gate, Easy walked her back to Dumbarton. They held hands and kept saying things about how crazy the fire was and how lucky they were to have gotten out before it took off, but the whole time they talked, the secret of what they had just shared was lingering right beneath the surface, and they kept exchanging sheepish, happy glances at each other.

"I love you," she whispered into his ear, standing on the marble steps of Dumbarton. It felt delicious to say it, and to know he was going to say it back.

He touched her chin and kissed her roughly on the forehead. "Love you, too."

She wished he could have stayed forever.

But he couldn't, as she had a dorm room and a roommate to go back to—one who wouldn't be too pleased to see her and Easy together. So she reluctantly parted from him and made her way upstairs. She pushed open the door to her room. Jenny was already changing into her pajamas, which were red waffle knit and covered with little goldfish. Callie smiled at the sight of her, still feeling on top of the world and flush with goodwill for everyone on the planet. She flopped down on her bed, enjoying the feel of her ultra-soft down comforter on her chilled legs. "God, that was totally insane, wasn't it?"

Jenny turned around to face her, a strange expression on her face. "What, you mean the fact that you've been lying to me all this time?" Her voice cracked at the end of her sentence, the way it did when she was about to cry, and Callie wondered if she was going to burst into tears. But she didn't.

Callie sat up in bed, confused. Why was everyone always mad at her all the time when she was just trying to be nice? "What are you talking about?"

Jenny's huge brown eyes almost bugged out of her head. "What about the pact we made—that both of us were going to put Easy behind us?" She shook her head slowly, her eyes not angry so much as puppy-dog sad. "Did that mean nothing to you?"

Callie stood up awkwardly. She was horrible at dealing with disappointment—even though she'd lived with her mother long enough to get good at it. Whenever someone told her she'd let them down, she couldn't help feel defensive. She strode over to her mirror and pretended to brush her hair, but really she was searching for hickeys. "I really don't understand what the big deal is." The words came out a little more icily than she wanted, but she wasn't going to back down. "I thought you'd moved on to Julian by now, anyway. You were all excited about him the other day."

"You don't even get it, do you?" Jenny's eyes flared up with anger and she stalked over to her dresser, not letting Callie avoid her. "It's not even about Easy. It's about *you*." Her voice softened as she played with her metal tray of barrettes, picking one up and then dropping it back into place. "I thought we were really friends now, but obviously I was wrong."

That pissed Callie off. They *were* friends—or at least, they had been until she had to go and get all judgmental on her. Callie narrowed her green eyes right at Jenny. "Don't you think this is a little ironic? *You* yelling at me for being with Easy, who was my boyfriend before you stole him away!"

Jenny gasped, reeling backward, her cheeks flushed with fury. "This is not about Easy!" she shouted.

"Funny," Callie spat back, tugging off her sweater and really hoping there weren't any hickeys in any other spots. It had felt like Easy was kissing every inch of her body an hour ago. "That's not what it sounds like."

"I can't believe I even expected you to be a *person* about this." Jenny threw back the covers to her bed and fluffed her pillow with vicious force. "I should have known better. And I guess I shouldn't be surprised, either, by the fact that you and Easy would be so stupid and selfish as to light the whole barn on fire with your gross smoking habit!"

It was Callie's turn to gape. She pulled on her pink-and-red-striped Ralph Lauren pajama top. "What are you talking about?" she demanded, feeling panicky. "We definitely did not start that fire."

"Really?" Jenny's hands were placed on her curvy hips. She looked ready to rip Callie's head off—or get her expelled or something. She'd never looked so passionate before. "Well, I saw the two of you in the barn, smoking. So it doesn't sound like it's that impossible."

"You *saw* us?" Callie gasped, tightening the drawstring bottoms around her slim hips. "Then how do I know *you* didn't start the fire to try and kill us because you were so jealous?" It suddenly made perfect sense to Callie. Jenny had started the fire and was only pretending to be upset about something else, when really she felt guilty and scared that she might get busted. "That sounds like motivation to me."

Jenny stuffed her feet into her thick crocheted slippers with the faux-shearling lining that looked like they'd been around since the eighties. "Yeah, it probably would." And then she flounced out the door, her curly boho braided hair bouncing behind her.

What was *that* supposed to mean?

OwlNet

BennyCunningham: That was so scary. I can't believe we almost, like, went up in flames. . . . I felt so vulnerable.

LonBaruzza: You were nowhere near the barn, you tease. You just like to be the damsel in distress.

BennyCunningham: Whatever. Still can't get over the sight of Callie and EZ running half-naked from the barn. So much for their secret affair.

LonBaruzza: You know the saying: there's no girlfriend like an ex-girlfriend! Think their flaming passion set the barn on fire?

BennyCunningham: Gross. Everyone knows they smoke like fiends. . . . I wouldn't be surprised. I hope they don't get expelled!!

LonBaruzza: Dunno. I saw Tinsley sneaking around back there too. Maybe she did it.

BennyCunningham: Hmph. Why were you watching HER?

LonBaruzza: Doesn't everybody?

OwlNet

AlanStGirard: Think Callie and EZ finally did the deed? They really got caught with their pants down!

HeathFerro: Pretty sad if Walsh couldn't manage to seal the deal. Had my money on him ending up w/Miss Boobs, tho.

AlanStGirard: Come to think of it . . . I DID see Jenny back there too. Think they had a threesome on?

HeathFerro: Insert H.F. in Walsh's spot, por favor.

AlanStGirard: Speaking of threesomes—you and Brett and Kara? Are they just lezzies or do you have something kinkier going on?

HeathFerro: Please. There's not a girl on campus not interested in going for a pony ride. . . .

AlanStGirard: What kind of answer is that?

HeathFerro: The only one you're getting.

SageFrancis: Wacked-out party. Don't even know how to begin to digest all the juicy shit that hit the fan. Can you believe our prefect is a lesbian?

AlisonQuentin: So what? Kara's hot. If I weren't into Alan, who knows, maybe I'd go for her.

SageFrancis: As if. You're as straight as they come.

AlisonQuentin: Did you see poor Brandon's new girlfriend making out with skeezoid Brian Atherton? HTF did that happen?

SageFrancis: Poor BB. Girls always seem to treat him like dirt. At least the ones he picks.

AlisonQuentin: Oh yeah? Are you volunteering to cheer him up?

SageFrancis: Maybe. But I don't know if I can date a guy who's prettier than me!

AlisonQuentin: BTW, did anyone watch the movie?

SageFrancis: What movie???

HAVING A TRUE FRIEND MEANS NEVER HAVING TO SAY YOU'RE SORRY—BUT A GOOD OWL SAYS IT ANYWAY.

Jenny stormed out of Dumbarton in her pajamas, wishing she had one of those rubber balls you're supposed to squeeze when you're stressed or frustrated or angry. She stomped down the stairs, her slippers padding softly against the marble, making her wish she still had her big, heavy boots on—she wanted to stomp and be loud and make noise. Although maybe that wasn't the best idea, as it was almost curfew. But she couldn't have stayed in her dorm room for one more second, not with Callie lying to her face and trying to make it not seem like a big deal because of Julian.

And then she sighed. *Julian.* Jenny paused for a second when her feet hit the first floor. In a different mood, she would have smiled at the sight of the broom closet where he'd once been hiding. Their kiss had been . . . unexpected. And awesome.

She almost giggled, thinking back at it, her mood starting to lift.

The door to Brett and Tinsley's door was open, but as Jenny peeked hesitantly inside, not wanting Tinsley to bite it off, she saw that it was empty. She padded over to Kara's room and knocked gently.

There was a pause and some shuffling before Kara appeared wearing a baggy Red Hot Chili Peppers concert T-shirt and a pair of black leggings.

"Hey," Jenny said, grateful to see a friendly face. "I was just looking for Brett."

"Oh, yeah." Kara opened the door further and saw Brett sitting in Kara's desk chair.

"What are you doing here?" Brett asked, her voice cold. Her short hair was pulled into two short pigtails at the side of her head, and her makeupless face looked kind of young and sad. She was wearing a pair of gray-striped flannel pajamas but seemed to be shivering inside them.

Jenny was taken aback. She paused where she was and looked at Brett blankly. "I, uh . . . You weren't in your room, so I figured you'd be here."

"Be a little louder, Jenny." Brett laughed hollowly, sounding completely unlike herself. "Although I guess you already told everyone everything anyway."

Jenny rushed toward her. "I did not tell anyone!" she whispered. "I would never do that to you." Tinsley could hate her all she wanted, and even Callie could want to murder her, but just the idea that Brett could be mad at her made Jenny want to dig a hole and bury herself in it. But Brett couldn't be mad at her for this—she hadn't done anything.

"No?" Brett asked, her voice wavering. She rubbed a hand across her face, looking completely forlorn.

Callie. It was all Callie and her stupid, drunkenly insinuating comments. Jenny bit her lip. "But I do think Callie knows . . . and I kind of heard her, well, implying things. To other people."

Brett covered her face in both hands. "I think I'm going crazy," she admitted despondently. Her green cat eyes turned to Jenny, looking wobbly and sad. "I'm so sorry, Jenny. I didn't meant to accuse you. I just . . . don't know what I'm doing right now." She tried to laugh but it came out as a hiccup. "I practically strangled Heath earlier when I thought it was him."

"It's okay," Jenny reassured her. Kara closed the door behind her and then plopped down on the bed. Jenny perched herself on the end, not sure if Brett wanted a hug or not. "But wait, how did Heath know about you guys?"

Brett chuckled weakly. "He sort of started it all." She smiled at Kara, who was sitting cross-legged with her pillow in her lap. It looked like the two of them were talking to each other across the room without even saying anything. "But it wasn't him that spilled it—we had this sort of deal."

Jenny was still a little confused, but she nodded anyway. "But . . . how did Callie know anything?"

Kara cleared her throat, and both girls turned to look at her. "About that." She looked sheepishly at Brett, squeezing the pillow to her chest. "I am so, so sorry—we just had this sort of bonding moment after the last meeting." Kara cringed, and her wide eyes started to fill with tears. "I didn't mean to tell her, it just sort of slipped out. This is all my fault."

Brett slid off the chair and sat down on the bed next to her. "It's okay." She smiled, and Jenny could tell she was trying to sound tougher than she felt. "At least we didn't burn the barn down."

To: Undisclosed recipients
From: DeanMarymount@waverly.edu
Date: Friday, October 11, 11:25 P.M.
Subject: Fire

Waverly Students,

As many of you know, there was a fire tonight at the Cinephiles party at the Millers' farm that resulted in the destruction of a seventy-year-old barn. Not only was this a completely irresponsible act, it was also incredibly dangerous and infantile. Whoever was responsible for starting the fire will be expelled from Waverly Academy immediately.

A disciplinary committee hearing will be scheduled for next week for all those present at the Cinephiles party. Your names are on record at the front office.

This is a deplorable abuse of the school's trust. Anyone who has information about the guilty party is morally and ethically required to report that information in immediately—at risk of expulsion.

Dean Marymount

A LOYAL OWL IS ALWAYS ON HIS GIRLFRIEND'S
SIDE—NO MATTER WHAT.

On Saturday morning, Callie was torn out of a deep sleep by the buzzing of her cell phone. She rubbed her eyes and squinted at the tiny screen. She had a new text message: *Get out of bed, lazybones. Meet me outside your dorm in 20, okay? Xo.* Callie smiled in spite of herself. It was like Easy couldn't bear to be out of her sight for too long. Good. That was how it should be.

When she'd gotten undressed last night, she'd found a piece of hay stuck in her sweater, and she'd slipped it into her desk drawer so that whenever she opened it, she would remember last night. She kind of wished she had a scrapbook, but then she realized it might be kind of weird to put something like that in there. She could picture her mom flipping through it and wanting to know why she had kept a piece of hay for posterity.

Callie glanced over at her roommate's bed, noticing it was

empty. Her sheets and blankets were twisted into a giant lump at the foot of the bed. Probably one way of saying eff you to Callie after their fight last night. Well, nice fucking try. Like she gave a shit if she left the room a mess—*Callie* left the room a mess. She flounced into the shower, resolved not to think any more about her self-righteous little roommate who needed to learn how to *get over it*.

After throwing on a pair of slim-fitting Stella McCartney jeans and her newest pair of boots—ultra-cozy black suede Michael Kors fur-lined ones that made her think of all the upcoming winter days that would be spent snuggling with Easy, with or without the boots on—she hurried outside, eager to walk into the dining hall with Easy on her arm and have the whole world know that finally, he was hers once again.

Take that, Ms. Humphrey.

Easy was waiting for her on the front steps. She paused before opening the door and going out to meet him. Through the window, she could see his outline against the brilliant blue sky, all the autumn leaves in full color. She'd never really gotten all the fuss about the leaves before. But right then, the beautiful colors seemed to be forming a perfect frame for the back of his head.

She opened the door slowly, and he spun around. "Hey," she said, a little awkwardly, stepping outside. Despite the sunny blue skies, it was freezing, and she was glad she'd decided to put on her cream-colored Ralph Lauren peacoat. She could feel her wet hair start to stiffen in the cold.

Easy still looked kind of sleepy, but unbelievably cute in his navy quilted vest and jeans. "Wanna go for a walk? I brought breakfast." She noticed two paper coffee cups sitting on the steps. He shook the bag in his hand. "Bagels."

Callie tried to hide her disappointment. She'd really been looking forward to walking into the dining hall together and having everyone see them, to establishing the way things were going to be from now on. But . . . it was pretty sweet of him to surprise her. She smiled. "What kind?"

"One cinnamon-raisin, extra-toasted, with fat-free cream cheese." His eyes glinted in the sunlight. "But that's for me."

Callie slapped her hand against his chest and he caught it, holding it for a second in his own calloused hand. At the touch of his skin, she felt her own starting to heat up again. "Where are we going to go?" she asked, a little huskily.

He picked up one of the cups of coffee and handed it to her, still steaming. She gratefully wrapped her hands around the warm cup, but was very conscious of the whiteness of her coat. It seemed to be begging her to spill all over it. "Maybe up to the bluffs?"

She hid her frown. *No one* would see them up there. But . . . whatever. Maybe that was the way he wanted it. They started out across the grass, their feet crunching noisily against the cold, colored leaves.

"Everyone's really talking about this fire," Easy said as they walked.

Callie glanced over at him. "Well, yeah. We don't have off-campus parties and burn down barns every day."

He took a sip of coffee, making a cute little noise as he

swallowed the hot liquid. Then he cleared his throat and glanced at her, his deep blue eyes looking troubled. "Well, I guess a lot of people kind of think we started it."

"What?!" Callie stopped walking. Of course Jenny was spreading rumors that the fire was their fault. "It's Jenny. I know it is. She's trying to get us expelled."

"What?" It was Easy's turn to be surprised. "Jenny? No way."

Callie stiffened up. Was he defending that little fire-starting ho-bag? She felt her palms start to sweat. Not again. "She saw us, you know. We had a huge fight last night, and she called me all these names." That wasn't exactly true, but Easy didn't really need to know the exact truth. He just needed to be on his girlfriend's side, unquestioningly.

Easy absentmindedly combed through his hair with his hand. "Well, I'm sure she's upset, and all."

Wrong answer. Callie took a step away from Easy and took a sip of her coffee. Almost immediately, she felt a few drips sneak out the plastic top of the cup and splatter against her coat. *Fuck.* "If you think she's so great, then maybe you should just go be with her right now."

"Don't be like that." Easy took two steps forward and quickly put his arms around her—the quickest response he'd ever had to one of her temper tantrums. Callie was impressed. He nuzzled his lips against her ear and Callie closed her eyes and forgot about the coffee that was probably going to stain her brand-new coat. His hoarse whisper tickled her ear deliciously. "You know last night was the best night of my life."

She sighed and pressed her lips to Easy's neck. That was more like it.

But he pulled away slightly. His forehead was furrowed with worry. His dry fingers traced her cheekbones.

"What is it?" she asked.

"I'm just worried. . . ." He stepped away from her and picked up a stick that was lying on the lawn and chucked it into the distance. "If I know Marymount—and after all the trouble I've been in, I think I do—someone's going to take the fall for this."

Callie grabbed his hand and squeezed it. She and Easy were finally back together. They were in love, just in time to drink hot cocoa after dinner together at night and kiss in the middle of the quad the first time it snowed. It wasn't going to be them. It *couldn't* be. And if that meant it had to be someone else, well, so be it.

 **Owl** Net

BennyCunningham: OMG. Did you hear? They found Julian's Zippo in the wreckage of the fire!!

TinsleyCarmichael: No kidding.

BennyCunningham: I guess he's the prime suspect. Hope he doesn't get expelled. He's too cute, even if he's a freshman.

TinsleyCarmichael: I actually SAW him behind the barn . . . with Jenny. Guess they've been hooking up. Think they started it?

BennyCunningham: Probably. There's something shifty about a guy that tall and a girl that's practically a midget.

TinsleyCarmichael: Totally . . .

CallieVernon: Hey. How are you?

TinsleyCarmichael: Um, fine.

CallieVernon: Sorry we haven't talked this week.

TinsleyCarmichael: Whatever.

CallieVernon: U in trouble for the barn? Because I think I know who did it.

TinsleyCarmichael: Talk to me, sister.

CallieVernon: Jenny. She saw me and EZ, um, together. Together, together.

TinsleyCarmichael: Sounds like motive to me.

CallieVernon: Exactly.

TinsleyCarmichael: I'm soooo on it. And Cal?

CallieVernon: Yeah?

TinsleyCarmichael: It's good to have you back on the dark side.

CallieVernon: Good to be here. Later, babe.

Once upon a time on the Upper East Side of New York City,
two beautiful girls fell in love with one perfect boy. . . .

Turn the page for a sneak peek of

it had to be you
the gossip girl prequel

and find out how it all began.

by the #1 *New York Times* bestselling author
Cecily von Ziegesar

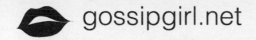
gossipgirl.net

topics ◄ *previous* *next* ► *post a question* *reply*

Disclaimer: All the real names of places, people, and events have been altered or abbre-viated to protect the innocent. Namely, me.

hey people!

Ever have that totally freakish feeling that someone is listening in on your conversations, spying on you and your friends, following you to parties, and generally stalking you? Well, they are. Or actually, *I* am. The truth is, I've been here all along, because I'm one of you.

Feeling totally lost? Don't get out much? Don't know who "we" are? Allow me to explain. We're an exclusive group of indescribably beauti-ful people who happen to live in those majestic, green-awninged, white-glove-doorman buildings near Central Park. We attend Manhattan's most elite single-sex private schools. Our families own yachts and estates in various exotic locations throughout the world. We frequent all the best beaches and the most exclusive ski resorts. We're seated immediately at the nicest restaurants in the chicest neighborhoods with-out a reservation. We turn heads. But don't confuse us with Hollywood actors or models or rock stars—those people you feel like you know because you hear so much about them, but who are actually completely boring compared to the parts they play or the songs they sing. There's nothing boring about me or my friends, and the more I tell you about us, the more you're going to want to know. I've kept quiet until now, but something has happened and I just can't stay quiet about it. . . .

the greatest story ever told

We learned in our first eleventh-grade creative writing class this week that most great stories begin in one of the following fashions: someone mysteriously disappears or a stranger comes to town. The story I'm about to tell is of the "someone mysteriously disappears" variety.

To be specific, **S** is *gone*.

In order to unravel the mystery of why she's left and where she's gone, I'm going to have to backtrack to last winter—the winter of our sophomore year—when the La Mer skin cream hit the fan and our pretty pink rose-scented bubble burst. It all started with three inseparable, perfectly innocent, über-gorgeous fifteen-year-olds. Well, they're sixteen now, and let's just say that two of them are *not* that innocent.

If anyone is going to tell this tale it has to be me, because I was at the scene of every crime. So sit back while I unravel the past and reveal everyone's secrets, because I know everything, and what I don't know I'll invent, elaborately.

Admit it: you're already falling for me.

Love you too . . .

gossip girl

the best stories begin with one boy and two girls

"Truce!" Serena van der Woodsen screamed as Nate Archibald body-checked her into a three-foot-high drift of powdery white snow. Cold and wet, it tunneled into her ears and down her pants. Nate dove on top of her, all five-foot eleven inches of his perfect, golden-brown-haired, glittering-green-eyed, fifteen-year-old boyness. Nate smelled like Downy and the Kiehl's sandalwood soap the maid stocked his bathroom with. Serena just lay there, trying to breathe with him on top of her. "My scalp is cold," she pleaded, getting a mouthful of Nate's snow-dampened, godlike curls as she spoke.

Nate sighed reluctantly, as if he could have spent all day outside in the frigid February meat locker that was the back garden of his family's Eighty-second-Street-just-off-Park-Avenue Manhattan town house. He rolled onto his back and wriggled like Serena's long-dead golden retriever, Guppy, when she used to let him loose on the green grass of the Great Lawn in Central Park. Then he stood up, awkwardly dusting off the seat of his neatly pressed Brooks Brothers khakis. It was Saturday, but he still wore the same clothes he wore every weekday as a sophomore at the St. Jude's School for Boys over on East End Avenue. It was the unofficial Prince of the Upper East Side uniform, the same uniform he and his classmates had been wearing since they'd started nursery school together at Park Avenue Presbyterian.

Nate held out his hand to help Serena to her feet. She frowned cautiously up at him, worried that he was only faking her out and was about to tackle her again. "I really am cold."

He flapped his hand at her impatiently. "I know. Come on."

She snorted, pretended to pick her nose and wipe it on the seat of her snow-soaked dark denim Earl jeans, then grabbed his hand with her faux-snotty one. "Thanks, pal." She staggered to her feet. "You're a real chum."

Nate led the way inside. The backs of his pant legs were damp and she could see the outline of his tighty-whiteys. Really, how gay of him! He held the glass-paned French doors open and stood aside to let her pass. Serena kicked off her baby blue Uggs and scuffed her bare, Urban Decay Piggy Bank-pink-toenailed feet down the long hall to the stately town house's enormous, barely used all-white Italian Modern kitchen. Nate's father was a former sea captain-turned-banker, and his mother was a French society hostess. They were basically never home, and when they *were* home, they were at the opera.

"Are you hungry?" Nate asked, following her. "I'm so sick of takeout. My parents have been in Venezuela or Santa Domingo or wherever they go in February for like two weeks, and I've been eating burritos, pizza, or sushi every freaking night. I asked Regina to buy ham, Swiss, Pepperidge Farm white bread, Grammy Smith apples, and peanut butter. All I want is the food I ate in kindergarten." He tugged anxiously on his wavy, golden brown hair. "Maybe I'm going through some sort of midlife crisis or something."

Like his life is so stressful?

"It's *Granny* Smith, silly," Serena informed him fondly. She opened a glossy white cupboard and found an unopened box of cinnamon-and-brown-sugar Pop-Tarts. Ripping open the box, she removed one of the packets from inside, tore it open with her neat, white teeth, and pulled out a thickly frosted pastry. She sucked on the Pop-Tart's sweet, crumbly corner and hopped up on the counter, kicking the cupboards below with her size-eight-and-a-half feet. Pop-Tarts at Nate's. She'd been having them there since she was five years old. And now . . . and now . . .

Serena sighed heavily. "Mom and Dad want me to go to boarding school next year," she announced, her enormous, almost navy blue eyes growing huge and glassy as they welled up with unexpected tears. Go away to boarding school and leave Nate? It hurt too much to even think about.

Nate flinched as if he'd been slapped in the face by an invisible hand. He grabbed the other Pop-Tart from out of the packet and hopped up on the counter next to Serena. "No way," he responded decisively. She couldn't leave. He wouldn't allow it.

"They want to travel more," Serena explained. The pink, perfect curve of her lower lip trembled dangerously. "If I'm home, they feel like they need to be home more. Like I want them around? Anyway, they've arranged for me to meet some of the deans of admissions and stuff. It's like I have no choice."

Nate scooted over a few inches and put his arm around her. "The city is going to suck if you're not here," he told her earnestly. "You can't go."

Serena took a deep shuddering breath and rested her pale blond head on his shoulder. "I love you," she murmured, closing her delicate eyelids. Their bodies were so close the entire Nate-side of her hummed. If she turned her head and tilted her chin just so, she could have easily kissed his warm, lovely neck. And she wanted to. She was actually dying to, because she really did love him, with all her heart.

She did? Hello? Since when?!

Maybe since ballroom-dancing school way back in fourth grade. She was tall for her age, and Nate was always such a gentleman about her lack of rhythm and the way she stepped on his insteps and jutted her bony elbows into his sides. He'd finesse it by grabbing her hand and spinning her around so that the skirt of her puffy, oyster-colored satin tea-length Bonpoint dress twirled out magnificently. Their teacher, Mrs. Jaffe, who had long blue hair that she kept in place with a pearl-adorned black hairnet, worshipped Nate. So did Serena's best friend, Blair Waldorf. And so did Serena—she just hadn't realized it until now. Serena shuddered and her perfect skin broke out in a rash of goose bumps. Her whole body seemed to be having an adverse reaction to the idea of revealing something she'd kept so well hidden for so long, even from herself.

Nate wrapped his lacrosse-toned arms around her long, narrow waist and pulled her close, tucking her pale gold head into the crook of his neck and massaging the ruts between the ribs on her back with his fingertips. The best thing about Serena was her total lack of embarrassing flab. Her entire body was as long and lean and taut as the strings on his Prince titanium tennis racket.

It was painful having such a ridiculously hot best friend. Why couldn't his best friend be some lard-assed dude with zits and dandruff? Instead he had Serena and Blair Waldorf, hands down the two hottest girls on the Upper East Side, and maybe all of Manhattan, or even the whole world.

Serena was an absolute goddess—every guy Nate knew talked about her—but she was mysterious. She'd laugh for hours if she spotted a cloud shaped like a toilet seat or something equally ridiculous, and the next moment she'd be wistful and sad. It was impossible to tell what she was thinking most of the time. Sometimes Nate wondered if she would've been more comfortable in a body that was slightly less perfect, because it would've given her more *incentive*, to use an SAT vocabulary word. Like she wasn't sure what she had to aspire to, since she basically had everything a girl could possibly want.

Blair was petite, with a pretty, foxlike face, blue eyes, and wavy chestnut-colored hair. She let everyone know what she was thinking, and she was fiercely competitive. For instance, she always found opportunities to point out that her chest was almost a whole cup size larger than Serena's and that she'd scored almost 100 points higher than Serena on the practice SAT.

Way back in fifth grade, Serena had told Nate she was pretty sure Blair had a crush on him. He started to notice that Blair did stick her chest out when he was looking, and she was always either bossing him around or fixing his hair. Of course Blair never admitted that she liked him, which made him like her even more.

Nate sighed deeply. No one understood how difficult it was being best friends with two such beautiful, impossible girls.

Like he would have been friends with them if they were awkward and butt-ugly?

He closed his eyes and breathed in the sweet scent of Serena's Frédéric Fekkai Apple Cider clarifying shampoo. He'd kissed lots of girls and had even gone to third base last June with L'Wren Knowes, a very experienced older Seaton Arms School senior who really did seem to know everything. But kissing Serena would be . . . different. He loved her. It was as simple as that. She was his best friend, and he loved her.

And if you can't kiss your best friend, who *can* you kiss?

upper east side schoolgirl uncovers shocking sex scandal!

"Ew," Blair Waldorf muttered at her reflection in the full-length mirror on the back of her closet door. She liked to keep her closet organized, but not too organized. Whites with whites, off-whites with off-whites, navy with navy, black with black. But that was it. Jeans were tossed in a heap on the closet floor. And there were dozens of them. It was almost a game to close her eyes and feel around and come up with a pair that used to be too tight in the ass but fit a little loosely now that she'd cut out her daily after-dinner milk-and-Chips-Ahoy routine.

Blair looked at the mirror, assessing her outfit. Her Marc by Marc Jacobs shell pink sheer cotton blouse was fine. It was the fuchsia La Perla bra that was the problem. It showed right through the blouse so that she looked like a stripper. But she was only going to Nate's house to hang out with him and Serena. And Nate liked to talk about bras. He was genuinely curious about, for instance, what the purpose of an underwire was, or why some bras fastened in front and some fastened in back. It was a big turn-on for him, obviously, but it was also sort of sweet. He was a lonely only child, craving sisterhood.

Right.

She decided to leave the bra on for Nate's sake, hiding the whole ensemble under her favorite belted black cashmere Lora Piano cardigan, which would come off the minute she stepped into his well-heated town house. Maybe, just maybe, the sight of her hot pink bra would be the thing to make Nate realize that he'd been in love with her just as long as she'd been in love with him.

Maybe.

She opened her bedroom door and yelled down the long hall and across the East Seventy-second Street penthouse's vast expanse of period furniture, parquet floors, crown moldings, and French Impressionist paintings. "Mom! Dad? I'm going over to Nate's house! Serena and I are spending the night!"

When there was no reply, she clomped her way to her parents' huge master suite in her noisy Kors wooden-heeled sheepskin clogs, opened their bedroom door, and made a beeline for her mom's dressing room. Eleanor Waldorf kept a tall stack of crisp emergency twenties in her lingerie drawer for Blair and her ten-year-old brother, Tyler, to parse from— for taxis, cappuccinos, and, in Blair's case, the occasional much-needed pair of Manolo Blahnik heels. Twenty, forty, sixty, eighty, one hundred. Twenty, forty, sixty, eighty, two hundred. Blair counted out the bills, folding them neatly before stuffing them into the back pocket of her peg-legged Seven jeans.

"If I were a cabernet," Blair's father's dramatically playful lawyer's voice echoed out of the adjoining dressing room, "how would you describe my bouquet?"

Excusez-moi?

Blair clomped out of her mom's dressing room and reached for the chocolate brown velvet curtain hanging in the doorway of her dad's. "If you guys are in there together, like, doing it while I'm home, then that's really gross," she declared flatly. "Anyway, I'm going over to Nate's, so—"

Her father, Harold J. Waldorf, Esquire, pulled aside the velvet curtain, dressed in his cashmere tweed Paul Smith bathrobe and nothing else, his nicely tanned, handsome face looking slightly flushed. "Mom's out looking at dishes for the Guggenheim benefit. I thought you were out. Where are you going exactly?"

Blair stared at him. He wasn't holding a phone, and if her mom was out, then who the fuck had he just been talking to? She stood blinking at him with her hands on her hips, tempted to peek inside his dressing room to see who he was hiding in there.

Does she really want to know?

Instead, she stumbled out of the master suite, clomped her way across the penthouse, grabbed her blood orange–colored Jimmy Choo treasure chest hobo, and ran for the elevator.

Outside it was breathtakingly cold, and fat flakes fell at random. Usually she walked the twelve blocks to Nate's house, but today Blair had no patience for walking—she had just discovered that her father was a lying, cheating scumbag, after all, and a cab was waiting for her downstairs. Or rather, a cab was waiting for Mrs. Solomon in 4A, but when the hunter green uniform–clad doorman saw the terrifying look on Blair's normally pretty face, he let her take it.

Besides, hailing cabs in the snow was probably the highlight of his day.

The stone walls bordering Central Park were blanketed in snow. A tall, elderly woman and her Yorkshire terrier, dressed in matching red Chanel quilted coats with matching black velvet bows in their white hair, crossed Seventy-second Street and entered the Ralph Lauren flagship store. Blair's cab hurtled recklessly up Madison Avenue, past Agnès B. and Williams-Sonoma and the Three Guys coffee shop where all the Constance Billard girls gathered after school, and finally pulled up to Nate's town house.

"Let me in!" she yelled into the intercom outside the Archibalds' elegant wrought-iron-and-glass front door as she swatted the buzzer over and over with her hand.

Inside, Nate and Serena were still cuddling in the kitchen. Serena raised her head from his shoulder and opened her eyes, as if from a dream. The kiss they'd both been fantasizing about had never actually happened, which was probably for the best.

"I think I'm warm now," she announced and hopped off the counter, composing her face so that she looked totally calm and cool, like they hadn't just had a moment. And maybe they hadn't—she couldn't be sure. She grinned at the monitor's distorted image of Blair giving her the finger. "Come on in, sweetness!" she shouted back, buzzing her friend in.

Nate tried to erase the disturbing thought that Blair had

caught him and Serena together. They weren't together. They were just friends, hanging out, which is what friends do when they're together. There was nothing to catch. It was all in his mind.

Or was it?

"Hey, hornyheads." Blair greeted them with snow in her shoulder-length chestnut brown hair. Her cheeks were pink with cold, her blue eyes were slightly bloodshot, and her carefully plucked dark brown eyebrows were askew, as if she'd been crying or rubbing her eyes like crazy. "I have a fucked-up story to tell you guys." She flung her orange bag down on the floor and took a deep breath, her eyes rolling around dramatically, milking the moment for all it was worth. "As it turns out, my totally boring, Mr. Lawyer father, Harold Waldorf, Esquire, is like totally having an affair. Only moments ago, I caught him asking some random babe, 'If I was a wine, how would you describe my bouquet?' and they were, like, totally hiding in his closet." She clapped her hand over her mouth, as if to keep the words in.

Or her breakfast.

"Whoa," Serena and Nate responded in unison.

"He just sounded so . . . slimy," Blair wailed through her fingers.

Serena knew this might be even grosser, but she just had to get it out there. "Well, maybe he was just having phone sex with your mom."

"Sure," Nate agreed. "My parents do that all the time," he added, feeling a little sick as he said it. His navy admiral dad was so uptight he probably wouldn't have phone sex for fear of being court-marshaled.

Blair grimaced. The idea of her tennis-toned-but-still-plump, St. Barts–tanned, gold-jewelry-loving mom having any kind of sex, let alone cabernet phone sex, with her skinny, preppy, argyle-socks-wearing dad, was so unlikely and so completely icky she refused to even think about it.

"No," she insisted, wolfing down the uneaten half of Serena's Pop-Tart. "It was definitely another woman. I mean, face it," she said, still chewing, "Dad is totally hot and dresses really well, and he's an important lawyer and everything. And my mom is totally insane and doesn't really do anything and she has varicose veins and a flabby ass. Of course he's having an affair."

Serena and Nate nodded their glossy golden heads like that made complete sense. Then Serena grabbed Blair and hugged her hard. Blair was the sister she'd never had. In fourth grade they'd pretended they were fraternal twins for an entire month. Their Constance Billard gym teacher, Ms. Etro, who'd gotten fired midyear for inappropriate touching—which she called "spotting"—during tumbling classes, had even believed them. They'd worn matching pink Izod shirts and cut their hair exactly the same length. They even wore matching gold Cartier hoop earrings, until they decided they were tacky and switched to Tiffany diamond studs.

Blair pressed her face into Serena's perfectly defined collarbone and heaved an exhausted, trembling sigh. "It's just so fucked up it makes me feel sick."

Serena patted Blair's back and met Nate's gaze over Blair's Elizabeth Arden Red Door Salon–glossed brown head. No way was she going to bring up the whole being-sent-away-to-boarding-school problem—not when her best friend was so upset. And she didn't want Nate to mention it either. "Come on, let's go mix martinis and watch a stupid movie or something."

Nate jumped off the counter, feeling completely confused. Suddenly all he really wanted to do was hug Blair and kiss away her tears. Was he hot for her now, too?

It's hard to keep a clear head when you're surrounded by beautiful girls who are in love with you.

"All we have is vodka and champagne. My parents keep all the good wine and whiskey locked up in the cabinet for when they have company," he apologized.

Serena slid open the bread pantry, where most families would actually keep bread, but where Nate's mom stored the cartons of Gitanes cigarettes her sister sent from France via FedEx twice a month because the ones sold in the States simply did not taste fresh.

"I'm sure we can make do," she said, ripping open a carton with her thumbnail. "Come." She stuck two cigarettes in her mouth like tusks and beckoned Nate and Blair to follow her out of the kitchen and upstairs to the master suite. If anyone was an expert at changing the mood, it was Serena. That was one of the things they loved about her. "I'll show you a good time," she added goofily.

She always did.

The Archibalds' vast bedroom had been decorated by Nate's mother in the style of Louis XVI, with a giant gilt mirror over the head of the enormous red-and-gold toile canopy bed, and heavy gold curtains in the windows. The walls were adorned with red-and-gold fleur-de-lis wallpaper and renderings of Mrs. Archibald's family's summer château near Nice. On the floor was a red, blue, and gold Persian rug rescued from the *Titanic* and bought at auction by Mrs. Archibald for her husband at Sotheby's.

"*Bus Stop*? *Some Like It Hot*? Or the digitally remastered version of *Some Like It Hot*?" Serena asked, flipping through Nate's parents' limited DVD collection. Obviously Captain Archibald liked Marilyn Monroe movies—*a lot*. Of course, Nate had his own collection of DVDs in his room, including a play-by-play of the last twenty years of America's Cup sailing races. Thanks, but no thanks. His parents' taste was far more girl-friendly. "Or we could just watch Nate play Nintendo, which is always hot," she joked, although she kind of meant it.

"Only if he does it naked," Blair quipped hopefully. She sat down and bounced up and down on the end of the huge bed.

Nate blushed. Blair loved to make him blush and he knew it. "Okay," he responded boldly, sitting down next to her on the bed.

Blair snatched a Kleenex out of the silver tissue box on Nate's mom's bedside table and blew her nose noisily. Not that she really needed to blow her nose. She just needed a distraction from the overwhelming urge to throw Nate down on his parents' bed and tackle him. He was so goddamned adorable it made her feel like she was going to explode. God, she loved him.

There had never been a time when she didn't love him. She'd loved the stupid lobster shorts he wore to the club in Newport when their dads played tennis together in the summer, back when they were, what—five? She'd loved the way he always had a Spider-Man Band-Aid on some part of his body until he was at least twelve, not because he'd hurt himself but because he thought it looked cool. She loved the way his whole head reflected the sunlight, glowing gold. She loved his glittering green eyes—eyes that were almost too pretty for a boy. She loved the way he so obviously knew he was hot but didn't quite know what to do about it. She loved him. Oh, how she loved him.

Oh, oh, *oh*!

She blew her nose with one last trumpeting snort and then grabbed a pink, tacky-looking DVD case from off the floor. She turned the case over, studying it. "*Breakfast at Tiffany's*. I've never seen it, but she's so beautiful." She held the DVD up so Serena could see Audrey Hepburn in her long black dress and pearl choker. "Isn't she?"

"She is pretty," Serena agreed, still sorting through the movies.

"She looks like you," Nate observed, cocking his head in such an adorable way that Blair had to close her eyes to keep from falling off the bed.

"You think?" Blair tossed her dirty tissue in the general direction of the Archibalds' dainty white porcelain waste paper basket and studied the picture on the DVD case again. In the movie that began to play in her head, she *was* Audrey Hepburn—a fabulously dressed, thin, perfectly coiffed, beautiful, mysterious megastar. "Maybe a little," she agreed, removing her black cashmere cardigan so that her hot pink bra was clearly visible beneath her blouse.

Blair picked up the DVD case again. Audrey Hepburn

looked so fabulous in the pictures on the back, but also sort of prim and proper, like she wore sexy underwear but wouldn't let a guy see it unless he was going to marry her. Blair pulled her cardigan back on and buttoned the top button. From now on, her life's work would be to emulate Audrey Hepburn in every possible way. Nate could see her underwear, but only once she was sure that one day they'd be married.

That makes sense—to her.

"I watched that movie with my mom," Nate confessed, causing both girls' hearts to drip into sticky puddles on the floor. "It's kind of bizarre, actually. I think it's supposed to be romantic, but I'm not sure I even understood it."

That was all the girls needed. Blair stuck the DVD into the player while Serena mixed martinis at the wet bar in the adjoining library. This involved pouring Bombay Sapphire into chilled martini glasses and stirring it with a silver letter opener. It was only 11 A.M.—not exactly cocktail hour—but Blair was in crisis, and Nate tended to take off his shirt when he got drunk. Besides, it was Saturday.

"There," Serena announced, as if she'd just put the finishing touches on a very complicated recipe. She handed out the glasses. "To us. Because we're worth it."

"To us," Blair and Nate chorused, glasses raised.

Bottoms up!

Before **Vanessa** filmed her first movie,
Dan wrote his first poem,
and **Jenny** bought her first bra.

Before **Blair** watched her first Audrey Hepburn movie,
Serena left for boarding school,
and before **Nate** came between them. . .

it had to be you
the gossip girl prequel

Coming October 2007

Blair Waldorf and Serena van der Woodsen
were the reigning princesses of the Upper East Side.

Until now.

Something wild and wicked is in the air.
The Carlyle triplets are about to
take Manhattan by storm.

Lucky for you, Gossip Girl will be there
to whisper all their juicy secrets. . . .

gossip girl

A New Era Begins
May 2008

the it girl

Popular Gossip Girl character Jenny Humphrey is leaving Constance Billiard to attend elite boarding school Waverly Academy, where the rich and glamorous students don't let the rules get in the way of an excellent time.

notorious

After a wild first week at boarding school, the Waverly student body can't help but whisper about Jenny and *her* body. But after getting expelled last year, the notorious Tinsley Carmichael is back, and she's not about to let some big-chested, rosy-cheeked city girl get all the attention. After all, there can only be *one* it girl.

reckless

The girls' dorm is put on lockdown, and being stuck in close quarters isn't helping ease the tension between Jenny, Callie, Brett, and Tinsley. Will the boys find a way to sneak in and party before the girls scratch one another's MAC mascara-ed eyes out?

unforgettable

After weeks of icy tension, roommates and romantic rivals Jenny and Callie decide to call a truce. But will the ceasefire *really* last, or will the dreamy Easy Walsh come between them yet again?

And keep your eye out for the fifth novel,
lucky, coming November 2007.

because I'm worth it

It's Fashion Week and the only place crazier than the fashion shows are the wild parties. Will Serena's sudden catwalk stardom make her new boyfriend seem totally last season?

I like it like that

It's spring break and the whole crew is heading to Sun Valley for some après-ski hot tub fun. With Nate playing knight-in-shining-armor to his crazy new girlfriend, Georgie, and Blair batting her eyelashes at Serena's brother Erik, the nights will be hot enough to stave off the mountain cold.

you're the one that I want

Mailboxes all over the Upper East Side are piling up with overstuffed envelopes from the Ivy League. Will who-got-in-where distract people from the more important question: Who's hooking up with whom?

nobody does it better

Spring is here and everyone is getting out of the house—and into the Plaza. Serena and Jenny are partying in the penthouse with New York's hippest band, The Raves, while Blair's taken up residence to get some alone time with Nate. And if posh hotel suites aren't plush enough, there's always Senior Spa Day!

nothing can keep us together

When Blair and Serena go head-to-head for the starring role in a major Hollywood movie, there's sure to be some drama worthy of the silver screen!

only in your dreams

It's the last summer before college, and love is in the air. Blair's off to London with her new British boyfriend—who's an awful lot like Nate. Nate's smooching beach babe Tawny—who's basically the anti-Blair. And Serena is half of Hollywood's hot new pairing—as if she wasn't smoldering on her own!

would I lie to you

Serena and Blair head to the Hamptons to be resident co-muses to the super-famous designer Bailey Winter, who just happens to live next door to Nate's beachside estate. So just how neighborly will these new neighbors get?

don't you forget about me

The countdown to college has officially begun! In just ten days, Blair, Serena, Nate, Vanessa, and Dan will bid adieu to New York's Upper East Side. The clock is ticking and that means three things: scandalous end-of-summer parties, now-or-never kisses, and one heart-breaking goodbye.

And keep your eye out for the Gossip Girl prequel, **it had to be you,** to find out how it all began. . . .

Coming October 2007

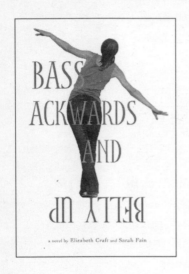
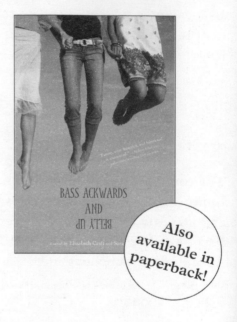